I tried the doorknob,

"Torie, do not go in that house," Rudy called out from the car window.

"I'll just be a minute." I was a bit worried about her, since she wasn't answering the door. If I entered and she was indecent, I would apologize until the cows came home, but if there was something wrong, she'd be eternally grateful. I took the chance and entered the house. "Maddie? It's me, Torie."

She wasn't in the living room or the kitchen, so I headed down the hallway toward the bedrooms. In the first bedroom on the left, I found Maddie lying on the floor with the phone knocked off the hook. Her face was locked in a horrible grimace, and spittle ran from her mouth. Her back arched, she was in the throes of some sort of seizure. "Oh, Jesus," I said. I flipped open my cell phone and called the sheriff's office directly.

"Mort, it's Torie. Get an ambulance out to Maddie Fulton's house right away, and I mean fast. Break the sound barrier if you have to."

---- ★ ----

Rett MacPherson

DIED
IN THE WOOL

W🌐RLDWIDE.®

TORONTO • NEW YORK • LONDON
AMSTERDAM • PARIS • SYDNEY • HAMBURG
STOCKHOLM • ATHENS • TOKYO • MILAN
MADRID • WARSAW • BUDAPEST • AUCKLAND

This book is for my husband
who lives with my little quirks—like never having enough
roses, or enough quilts, or enough fabric, or enough
books—and manages not to complain, too much. And who
at the end of the day still considers me "his woman."

And for the amazing women on my family tree who passed
the love of quilts and quilting down to me either through
their written record or through the record of their craft.

DIED IN THE WOOL

A Worldwide Mystery/April 2008

First published by St. Martin's Press, LLC.

ISBN-13: 978-0-373-26634-0
ISBN-10:   0-373-26634-0

Printed in U.S.A.

Acknowledgments

The author wishes to thank some people, as usual.

My writer's group: Tom Drennan, Laurell K. Hamilton, Martha Kneib, Debbie Millitello, Sharon Shinn, and Mark Sumner. You guys have been such great cheerleaders for Torie and her gang.

My editor, Kelley Ragland, and everybody at St. Martin's Press. My agent, Merrilee Heiftez, at Writers House.

Darla Cook for doing a lot of hand holding.

For the ladies at the Quilted Fox and Quilters Cottage. I feel inspired just being around them, their amazing quilts and the fantastic fabrics.

My kids, for keeping me sane, but not too sane. That would ruin all the fun.

ONE

IT WAS SPRINGTIME IN NEW KASSEL. As much as I love winter and snow, I always love to see spring come, bringing baby rabbits, lilacs, and birds busy at the feeders. It was the month of May, and our first annual New Kassel Garden Club rose show was about to kick off, and I was overseeing all of the festivities. Which would be interesting since the only thing I can really tell you about roses is that you stick them in the ground and they come up in pink, red, yellow, and white. I didn't really need to know a lot about roses, though. I just needed to know about making the tourists happy. The garden club would worry about the roses.

I, Torie O'Shea, wear several hats in this town. I used to work as a tour guide for Sylvia and Wilma Pershing, who had owned the Gaheimer House. Now I *own* the Gaheimer House. Sylvia left it to me when she passed away last year. I'm also a genealogist and serve on the Events Committee and am the president of the historical society. I have transcribed more Granite County records than I care to think about. The level of activity comes and goes. For several weeks I'll be in a frenzy trying to get everything prepared for a particular event, and then I'll have weeks and weeks of nothing much to do except to give tours of the Gaheimer House.

As much as I love the Gaheimer House and know every nook and cranny, I was beginning to feel the faintest flutter of boredom. I know, I know, it's something I never thought would happen to me—and can I just say that I think it's uniquely American that I could be both overwhelmed and bored all in the same month. I live and breathe this town and everything in it, but there was a part of me that longed to learn everything I could about a *new* place.

That's why when Helen Wickland entered my office at the Gaheimer House with the news that the old Kendall house was now on the market, I almost swallowed the cap on my pen.

"I swear," Helen said, crossing her heart. Helen is a dear friend of mine, a decade older than I am with more salt than pepper in her hair. She's lived in this town longer than I have. She's also the resident chocolatier. Oh yes, everyone should be best friends with the local chocolatier. It definitely has its perks. "I just heard it from Elmer."

Elmer Kolbe is the honorary fire chief. He got too old to work, so we made him retire, but he shows up to work every day anyway. "Really?" I asked.

"Just the other day you said that you wished Evan Merchant would finally put the Kendall house up for sale," she said. "Remember? You said it was an eyesore and that you wanted to buy it?"

"Well, it is," I said. "Sort of. Merchant doesn't keep up with the repairs and the painting, and sometimes he doesn't even mow the grass for, like, a month."

"Well, he's put it up for sale, and get this—he's selling off the contents, too," she said, beaming. "So if there are a few things inside that you'd like to buy for the Gaheimer House, you're about to get your wish."

"Incredible," I said. "How much are they asking for it?"

"I don't know," she said. "Are you seriously thinking about buying it? I mean, it's one thing to say you'd like to buy it, but it's another to actually buy it."

"If they're not asking an arm and a leg for it, I'm game."

Her eyes twinkled with anticipation, because she knew exactly what I'd do with the old Kendall house. Legend has it that a banker from up north by the name of Byron Kendall fell in love with the Mississippi river valley when he came through on his way to Kentucky during the Civil War. Supposedly, he'd vowed that if he made it through the war alive and the country was still intact, he was going to return and settle here. He did just that.

When he died in 1902, he left the house to his oldest son, Sanders. Sanders "Sandy" Kendall then raised his family of three in it. Everybody around here knows the name of Sandy Kendall because of the tragedy that befell him and his family. His wife died shortly before World War I. Then his oldest son fought in the trenches in Europe. A few years after that son came home from the Great War, all three Kendall children committed suicide in the house. It was a legend known throughout the Mississippi valley, and it would make one hell of a tourist trap.

"It would be New Kassel's newest attraction," I said. Helen smiled. "Not just for the revenue it would bring the town, but because I've wanted to tell the story of the Kendall children for a long time."

"So you'd set up tours?"

"You bet," I said. "You know, they say that the inside of the house is pretty much as it was when Sandy Kendall died."

"I know. I remember as a kid peeking through the slats

on the windows," she said. "Did Evan ever live in the main house?"

"I'm not sure," I said. "I'll have to ask him when I see him, but I'm fairly certain he's always lived in the guesthouse."

"Hmph," she said, working her lower lip with her fingers. "Seems odd."

"Nothing about that house or that family is normal," I said. "Do you know what's in that house?"

She shook her head.

"Supposedly all of Lieutenant Kendall's Civil War papers and uniforms, and his granddaughter's quilts. I can't remember her name, but she was a world-renowned quilter. I think I remember Sylvia saying that the girl's quilts had been shown at one of the World's Fairs and one was even in the Smithsonian."

"Wow," Helen said.

"It would make an excellent exhibition," I said.

"They're probably asking a bundle for it," she said.

"You're probably right," I said, "but it won't hurt to find out."

The back door to the Gaheimer House burst open just then and a loud, shrill voice yelled out, "Torie! You have got to do something about that woman!" My ears told me the visitor was Eleanore Murdoch long before she actually entered my office. Helen sat down in the chair across from my desk and rolled her eyes. Eleanore appeared in my doorway, huffing and puffing and clearly upset. Her ears were blood red, and Eleanore's ears only turn blood red when she is extremely peeved.

Eleanore owns the Murdoch Inn with her husband, Oscar, and has a little gossip column in the local newspaper. She's top-heavy and wears the most outrageous combinations of clothes, loud jewelry, and bright colors I've ever seen on a mammal. Today, I'm assuming in honor of spring, she wore a grass-green shirt with giant pink tulips appliquéd across the bottom of it. Her pants were bright gold tucked into green socks. Her purple and pink tennis shoes looked a bit out of place, but my guess was that she didn't have any yellow or green shoes. On her ears, she sported hummingbird earrings that looked as though the birds were about ready to take a drink from her neck. She didn't wear a hat with this ensemble, so I was a bit disappointed. "What can I do for you, Eleanore?"

"Maddie Fulton has got to be put in her place," she said. "First of all, the rose is not a superior flower to the clematis, but I let her have her way. Are we having a first-ever annual clematis show? No, siree. We're having a stupid rose show. *Now* she won't even listen to my gentle suggestions as to which roses should be in the show!"

Helen smiled and smothered a laugh. I wasn't laughing, though, because I knew that once Eleanore got on to something…Well, let's just say Eleanore is not unlike me in that she is a bit tenacious when it comes to something she believes in. Also, although the things I find important are quite often worlds apart from what Eleanore finds important, we both react sort of the same way about things, and that could spell trouble for everybody involved. She's much more obnoxious about it than I am, though. At least I hope so.

"Hybrid teas, Torie. That's what she should be focusing on. But no, she has no less than twelve floribundas, for heaven's sake. And don't even get me started on the Noisettes. And the few hybrid teas that she's picked, well, they're just not worthy," she said. "And she thinks David Austin is the Rose God or something."

Eleanore might as well have been the teacher in a Charlie Brown cartoon, because all I heard was *blah blah rose blah blah blah.* I had no clue what she was talking about, so I honestly didn't know if there had been a horticultural travesty committed or not. A rose is a rose is a rose, right? "Eleanore," I said.

"Who is the president of the New Kassel Garden Club, anyway?" she asked.

I started to answer but didn't get the chance.

"I'll tell you who," she said. "Dudley Froelich, that's who. And who is the vice president of the garden club?"

Tobias Thorley, but I didn't get to say so.

"Tobias Thorley," she said. "Not Maddie Fulton! Maddie Fulton does not hold an office in the garden club!"

"But," Helen spoke up, "Maddie is the resident rosarian, is she not?"

What the hell was a rosarian?

Eleanore got quiet a moment. "There are three other rosarians in town."

"Yes, but everybody knows Maddie is the woman you go to when you have problems with roses," Helen said. "Have you seen her garden? It's absolutely amazing."

Eleanore lifted her chin a notch. "I don't recall that I was addressing you, Helen," she said. "Torie, you must do something."

Helen made a face at Eleanore behind her back and acted like she was about ready to kick her in the pants. This made me laugh, which completely incensed Eleanore. "Sylvia would have done something!"

"Well, Eleanore," I said, "this has been discussed many times in the past. I am not Sylvia. What exactly is it you want me to do?"

"Tell her that...as Events Committee chairperson, you feel that her selection of roses is out of the question," she said. Her ears were getting redder, if that was possible, and her hummingbird earrings clanked around so much that I just knew the sides of her neck were going to be bruised.

"But that would be a lie," I said.

"Oh, like you've never lied before," she said, and crossed her arms.

"But I don't know the first thing about roses."

"When has your lack of knowledge ever stopped you from sticking your nose in?" she asked.

Okay, take a deep breath. I really had no reason to get upset, since Eleanore was speaking the truth. I have lied to get information before. On more occasions than I care to confess. Usually there was somebody's life hanging in the balance—and the fact that I can actually say that I've had to lie to save somebody's life really says a lot about the sad state of my own life. I've butted my nose into things without knowing all the facts, too. But damn, she didn't have to just blurt it out like that. Somebody might be listening. "I wouldn't know if she picked bad roses or not, Eleanore."

"I am telling you that she has. What, my word means nothing?"

Well, actually, no, but I wasn't going to say that.

She took a deep breath, and I held my hands up in desperation. "Eleanore, please. I'll talk to Maddie," I said, "but I don't know what good it's going to do."

"You just tell her that she's picked inappropriate and ugly roses."

"No rose is ugly," Helen said.

"Well, of course not," Eleanore said. "I'm exaggerating to get my point across."

"I'll talk to her," I said. "I'm just not making any promises. Because I can't."

"Fine," Eleanore said. "I also wanted to let you know that I am going to buy the Kendall house. They've just put it on the market."

I glanced at Helen. Panic had seized my friend. She began mouthing "no way" to me and shaking her head. "W-what are you going to do with it?" I asked.

"I'm going to turn it into one of those murder-mystery dinner theaters," she said. "It's not every day you get to have dinner in the house where three people killed themselves."

"Right," I said. "I guess that's an incentive to eat food."

"I'm off," Eleanore said, and whirled around on her heel and exited through the back door.

Helen and I stared at each other. Finally, Helen swallowed and spoke. "You cannot let that woman buy the Kendall house," she said.

"Why not? Helen, if she puts in a better bid than Rudy and I, she gets it," I said.

"It'll be cheesy," she said.

"No, murder-mystery dinners are fun," I said.

"Yes, but Eleanore will make it cheesy," she said.

"Now, she has pretty good taste when it comes to decorating the Murdoch Inn. *Midwest Living* did a small article on her bed-and-breakfast last fall when they covered the most quaint places to stay in seven states. Remember that?"

Helen stood then. "Whatever, Torie. But if Eleanore gets the Kendall house, I'm moving."

I knew Helen was exaggerating, but only just. "I don't know, Helen. Maybe what this town needs is something goofy and fun like a murder-mystery theater. Maybe me turning the Kendall house into a shrine for the dead is the wrong thing."

"The wrong thing? Torie, are you feeling all right? You are all about shrines for the dead."

"Gee, Helen," I said. "That makes me sound like I belong in the Norman Bates family or something."

"Think about it," she said. "You don't want Eleanore in charge of something like a mystery theater with nobody to curb her…enthusiasms."

I only smiled.

"Remember the time she decided to host a bird-watching expedition? She showed up looking like a giant version of Heidi. She got bit by a snake—and lived."

"But the snake died," I said laughing.

"I *know!* Then one of the birders got attacked by a flock of starlings and tried to sue the mayor for allowing the bird expedition in the first place," she said. I was laughing so hard my eyes were watering. "What about the time she had the pancake bake-off and blew up the ovens at the Knights of Columbus hall?"

"God, Elmer wouldn't speak to her for, like, six months," I said.

"Then there was the summer that she decided to learn how to skateboard, and then thought that the whole town should have a weekly skateboard-to-work day. Tobias broke a hip, and Colin had to write all those tickets for endangering the tourists!"

I was laughing so hard I could barely breathe.

"If she is in charge of a mystery theater, somebody will get killed. Simple as that."

"You're right, of course," I said, "but it's not against the law to open a business in this town, unless it's a house of ill-repute."

"Just promise me you will bid higher than she does."

"We'll see. It may be out of my financial ball park," I said, "but I will do all in my power to purchase the Kendall house."

"Thank you, God," she said, looking toward the ceiling. "See you later."

"Right," I said. "I'm off to see Maddie Fulton."

TWO

MADDIE FULTON LIVES just on the outskirts of town. I had every intention of going straight to her place, but decided to make a detour to the Kendall house. I couldn't help myself. Not only am I nosy by nature, but I'm also impatient as heck. For the record, New Kassel is a fairly small town; the population is under a thousand. It's nestled on a slight cliff overlooking the Mississippi River, about forty minutes to an hour south of St. Louis, depending on whether your destination is St. Louis city or St. Louis County. Granite County is mostly rural and used to be full of small family farms. Those are slowly but surely disappearing and giving way to the newest and brightest subdivisions, with homes on lots barely bigger than the foundations of the houses themselves. Not only does it break my heart to see the loss of the family farms, but the destruction of our wildlife habitat is catastrophic.

I turned down Haggeman Road, at the far west end of town. About seven houses down was the old Kendall house. Chipped paint flaked away from the multitude of windows that covered the front of the two-story Victorian. It had been painted a light yellow about fifteen years ago—I remember it well because Sylvia, Wilma, and I were all excited that the house was getting a face-lift—and the trim and windows had been done in forest green. A large front porch wrapped nearly all the way around the house, but stopped just short of it at the side door. A swing hung from one end of the porch, and a beautiful purple-flowering vine of some sort climbed all over the other end. A rather enormous tree—possibly oak—shaded half of the house with its leaf-smothered branches.

There was a blue Honda parked in the driveway, so Evan Merchant was most likely home. I parked, got out of the car, and made my way back to the guesthouse. The guesthouse was nothing to sneeze at by most people's standards. It was a nice, cozy bungalow, probably two bedrooms, situated behind the main house and virtually invisible from the street.

I knocked on the door, and after a moment, Evan Merchant answered. He was close to fifty, fit and trim with a head full of red hair. "Hi," I said. Just as I put my hand out to shake his, a little bitty dog ran between Evan's legs and began barking at me as if I were Ted Bundy. "Bon, shut up," Evan said.

"I'm Torie O'Shea," I said.

"Yes, I remember you," he said. "Come in."

His house was bright and airy and did not come across as a bachelor pad in the least. Well, except for the big flat-screen TV tuned to ESPN. Otherwise, as you could tell from the salmon-colored carpet and the vases sitting around full of floral arrangements, he had embraced his feminine side. "What can I do for you?" he asked.

"Um, well, I heard that you were putting the Kendall house up for sale," I said.

"That's right," he said. "You can go through my real estate agent. Hannah Sharpe, over in Wisteria."

"So it's official," I said.

"Oh, hell yes, it's official," he said. He seemed pretty anxious to get rid of the house, which meant I could have a really good chance of getting it before summer was out. I didn't know Evan Merchant very well. I'd seen him occasionally in town; he usually showed up for the bluegrass festival we hold once or twice a year. As far as I could remember, he worked somewhere up in South St. Louis. Don't ask me why, but the townsfolk who drive all the way to St. Louis for work stick out in my mind. "I want to close by July first."

Wonderful. I'd have a few months of good weather to do repairs before winter set in. Of course, I hadn't discussed any of this with my husband, Rudy, but it wouldn't hurt to have an idea of what I'd need to do if I did get the chance to buy the house.

I cleared my throat. Bon, the killer Chihuahua, spun around in circles and barked again. Evan shot the dog a look, and Bon jumped on the couch and shut up. If he could get that sort of respect out of a dog, why couldn't I get it out of my kids? If I shot Mary a look like that, she'd laugh at me. Of course, Mary is on the verge of being an Evil Teenager. I firmly believe the years between ten and fourteen are the worst. At least for the parent. And for the other siblings. Well, for any living being who has the unfortunate luck of being in the vicinity of somebody that age.

"Bon is an unusual name for a dog," I said.

"Oh, I named him after Bon Scott. The original lead singer for AC/DC."

"Right," I said. "Didn't he drink himself to death?"

"Yup," he said. "The dog sounds just like him." Evan

tilted his head to the side as he looked at the dog on the couch. Bon mirrored his movement. "Sorta looks like him, too," he said, and laughed.

"I was actually curious about the contents of the house. I heard you were planning on having an estate sale," I said.

"That's right," he said. "Boy, news travels fast in this town."

"You have no idea," I said.

"You want a Coke? Tea? I might have some Budweiser," he said.

"No, I'm fine," I said, following him into the kitchen. "I'd be really interested in the quilts and anything pertaining to fabric art. I think they would make an excellent display in town. A collection of fabric and needlework from historical women of the area would be a splendid addition to the Gaheimer Collection."

"Yeah," he said, grabbing a beer for himself from the fridge. "I think I remember seeing some old blankets in the house."

I handed him my card with my office, home, and cell phone numbers on it. "I would give you a very, very generous price for the whole collection of needlecrafts."

"Oh, yeah?" he said and took a drink. "Maybe it should go to auction if you think it's worth so much."

"Whatever you decide, I'm sure it would be fair," I said, "but I really think it's important that the quilts go to a historical society or a museum so that they don't end up in somebody's camping gear. I can guarantee them a good home, and I'm prepared to purchase them right away if you're in need of money now."

His eyes lit up then. Damn, I was good.

"Yeah," he said. "Let me talk it over with my lawyers and I'll get right back to you."

"Thank you so much," I said.

Evan showed me to the door. As I stepped out into the brilliant sunlight and saw the back of that wonderful home, I couldn't help but ask the inevitable question. "Evan, why have you never lived in the big house?"

He turned a bit pale then, especially around the mouth. "I did live in that house once. For about a week. The damn thing is haunted." I laughed until I realized he was serious. "Every night, I'd hear gunshots that weren't there. Crashing noises. The final straw was when I saw her…"

"Her?"

"The woman, young and so beautiful. She sat down on the edge of my bed and told me in a very polite way that I was sleeping in her bed and then asked if I would please retire to one of the other bedrooms in the house."

I laughed even harder. "Oh, Evan. There's no such thing as ghosts. You know, every single time I've thought a house was haunted, there was always a logical explanation for it. Everybody should watch Scooby-Doo. The Scooby gang would always think they had a ghost or zombie or whatever, and then they always found out it wasn't."

"Fine," he said. "Bring the Scooby gang over to check it out. Because that house is haunted. My dog won't go near it. He barks at the house all the time. And there's a room…upstairs." He shivered. "I was gonna paint it, but I got too spooked before I could get around to doing it. The good thing is that the ghosts seem to be confined to the house. They can't get out."

"How do you know?" I asked. As if they were real.

"I see her up there in that window all the time," he said, pointing to one of the second-floor windows. "She stares down at me. Places her hand on the glass like she wants out. But she never comes."

Chills danced down my spine. "Okay, well, let me know about the quilt collection, and I'll be in touch with your real estate agent."

I was halfway to my car when I remembered something else. "Evan, why didn't you just move?"

"Couldn't afford to until now. I would have lost my butt if I'd sold it in the first five years. Then, well, I got laid off, and I'd taken out a second and a third mortgage…you know," he said.

"Yeah, I understand," I said. "What kind of vine did I see on that gorgeous front porch?"

If it was possible, Evan Merchant's pallor got even worse. "Morning glories," he said.

"Morning glories," I said. "But it's after noon. I thought they only bloomed in the morning."

"Lady, morning glories are annuals, too. You know what that means?"

"Uhhh, they bloom once?"

"No, you have to plant them every year. They don't make it through the winter."

"So?"

"I've never replanted them. They come up every year. I've even gone over there and pulled them up by the roots. They come back, and they bloom all morning, all afternoon, and sometimes late at night they're still open."

I didn't know what to say to him. Surely he had to be

mistaken. There must be some weird breed or species of morning glories that bloomed all day and came back every year. Of course, then they'd be called "all-day glories." Still, there had to be some logical explanation for the flowers.

"Her name was Glory."

"Who was named Glory?" I said.

"The woman in the house. Her name was Glory Kendall."

THREE

As I was leaving Evan Merchant's house, I decided to head down to Debbie's Cookie Cutter and buy some chocolate chip cookies. I can honestly say that I believe I'd either be dead or in the nuthouse if it weren't for chocolate chips. Chocolate chip cookies, chocolate chip ice cream, chocolate chip muffins…I mean, as far as I'm concerned, there really isn't much need for other food. Okay, except pizza. I get really cranky if I go too long without an injection of chocolate chips. At least I haven't started carrying a bag of them around with me.

I bought two dozen chocolate chip cookies from Debbie and ran into the new sheriff of New Kassel on the street outside. "Mort," I said.

"Torie, what's up?"

Mort Joachim is younger than I am, probably about thirty-one or thirty-two. He'd only been sheriff for about six months. The position had been vacated by my stepfather, Colin Brooke, who had gone on to greener pastures as the town's mayor. I used to complain about the old mayor quite a bit. Then I found out he was actually a mobster living under an alternate identity. Sort of like a round, bald, bowling-obsessed villain in a comic book. Well, the new mayor, my stepfather, doesn't spend a lot of time bowling—except his usual Tuesday night league with my husband—but he spends countless hours golfing, since there really doesn't seem to be that much to do as mayor. I wish I'd known that, because I definitely would have run against him.

At any rate, the blond-haired, violet-eyed new sheriff was as green as grass and rather friendly. He had won his office against Lou Counts, the closest thing to Satan I'd ever come across. She is ex-military, driven, and no-nonsense, and she hates me with a passion. Unfortunately she is now a deputy for the sheriff's department, but I rarely have to have anything to do with her. I mostly deal with Mort, since I'm a special consultant to the sheriff—another one of those hats I wear.

"I was just headed home, Mort. How about you?"

"Tobias claims somebody dug up one of his rosebushes and did something with his gnomes."

"Oh, yeah, Tobias loves his garden gnomes," I said.

"So I'm headed over to investigate the vandalism," he said.

"Hey, Mort, I was wondering…you think you could check out the Kendall house for me?"

"What do you mean?" he asked.

"Just go over, check the locks, maybe make sure the windows haven't been broken into or anything," I said.

"Why?"

"Well, Evan Merchant claims the house is haunted. Of course, that's just not possible, but he says he sees a girl up in one of the windows, so I'm thinking maybe some squatters have taken up residence."

"I'll check it out," he said.

"Can you let me know what you find?"

"Sure."

Just then my cell phone rang. "I gotta take this," I said,

and waved to him. It was my husband calling. "Hey, Rudy, what's up?"

"Mary decided to use hair spray on the horses' manes," he said.

Well, any sentence that begins with "Mary decided," especially one that comes over a cell phone, is one to worry about, so my eyes had started rolling before he'd even finished this one. "What do you mean, she used hair spray?"

"She decided that she wanted the horses to have big hair. Like back in the eighties and nineties. She said Cutter looks like Jon Bon Jovi."

"Okay, here's the deal. Ground her from the hair spray, then tell her she has to wash it out of the manes herself. Then…hell, I don't know. Tell her she's on stall duty for the next month."

"You seriously want Mary to clean out the horses' stalls for the next month? We'll have horse manure everywhere," he said.

"I didn't say I wouldn't go and clean up behind her, but she needs to think she's cleaning the stalls."

"Oh," he said. "Do you always think this deviously, or only when it comes to our kids?"

"I'm not answering that," I said and laughed.

"What do you want for dinner?" he asked.

"I don't know. If there's nothing thawed, then I guess we're going with pasta," I said.

"How about I make some black beans and rice?" he said.

"Good," I said. "I'll be home in a few minutes. I need to pick up Rachel from rehearsal. You've got Matthew already, right?"

"Right," he said.

I had to check, because one time we were just sitting down to eat dinner when we realized that neither one of us had retrieved Matthew from my mother's. I wouldn't have felt so bad about this if Matthew was a quiet kid, a child that you could forget was there, but Matthew talks incessantly and is constantly blowing things up in his mind, so there's usually a fair amount of spit flying through the air at all times. You'd think we would notice that there wasn't a little boy jumping around the kitchen with his light saber making lots of spit noises, but we hadn't. I felt so horrible that I'd driven right over and gotten him without eating my dinner.

Well, everybody's forgotten his or her kid at least once. Right? Most of the time I can tell someone is missing when the decibel level in the house has changed by just a fraction. I'm usually very tuned in to what my children are doing, especially when they're out of the room. It's that Mommy Sense. I guess I had just been preoccupied that night, and, to be fair, each of us had assumed the other one had picked him up. Nevertheless, it was the low point of my maternal career, but worth several packages of Yu-Gi-Oh cards and at least one Teenage Mutant Ninja Turtle action figure for Matthew. He came out pretty good on the deal. In fact, Mary had asked if I could forget about her a few times.

I picked up Rachel from play practice at school. Her boyfriend, Riley, waved to us as we pulled out of the parking lot. Rachel is old enough to drive now, but she's sort of short and panics easily, so I'm not real thrilled with the idea.

Later, at dinner, Rachel wouldn't shut up. You must understand that there is absolutely nothing unusual about this, but Mary was fast losing her patience, as she had tried to speak at least three times.

Mary is a talker, too. She talks at such amazing speeds that sometimes I worry about her lips burning off. One of the kids at school told her she should become the "prices may vary" person. Yup, that person at the end of the commercials that comes on and says, "Prices may vary…" and then spews out this long tirade of disclaimers so fast that you can barely understand them. There's a reason for Mary's linguistic velocity. If she didn't speak quickly, Rachel would be talking again and Mary would never get anything said.

So, after ten minutes of listening to Rachel drone on and on about what person was playing what part in the play and how *amazing* each and every actor was, Mary lost all sense of propriety and let out a burp that rattled the walls. Rachel took one look at Mary and said, "Pig," and then just glared.

It was during that glaring moment that Mary cupped her hand to her ear. "Do you hear that?" Mary asked. "Silence."

Rachel stuck her tongue out at Mary.

"Jenny Abraham tried to kill herself," Mary said.

"What?" I asked.

"Yeah, she's, like, fifteen. I've been trying to tell you this for, like, the last twenty hours, but motormouth over there wouldn't give me a chance."

"Her mother must be devastated," I said.

"Why did she do it?" Rudy asked.

Mary shrugged. "Who knows?" she said.

"Well, is she all right? Is she at home or in the hospital?" I asked.

"She's fine. I think she's still at the hospital, though," Mary said, making designs on her plate with the black beans. Then she looked to Rachel. "You can continue with all that crap none of us care about now."

"So," Rachel said, "Mr. Zozlowski thought Deanna would make a better Juliet, but after watching Melinda, I'm telling you, Melinda owns the part. She is Juliet."

We all just stared at her. "What?" she asked, shoving her fork in her mouth.

The phone rang then, and I answered it on the second ring. "Hello," I said.

"Yeah, is this Torie O'Shea?"

"Yes," I said.

"Hi, it's Evan Merchant," he said. "I'd like to sell you those blankets and things."

"Great," I said. "Look, I'm going to call a local appraiser. I want this to be a fair deal. She'll come out and look at the quilts and let you know what they're worth."

"Okay," he said.

"She'll need to get in the house and see the quilts, though."

"That's fine," he said. "You going to be with her?"

"Probably."

"Good, then I don't need to be."

"Right," I said.

"Call me when she's available."

"I will," I said.

Later, after dinner and Matthew's bath—which is always a drenching event—I called Geena Campbell, the appraiser, who lives in St. Louis. I've known Geena for a few years now. We have some quilts in the Gaheimer Collection, and I had inherited a few of my own family heirloom quilts. In fact, a few years back, I started quilting. I'm not very good, and it takes me forever to finish one. I always have more ideas than actual projects, and I've bought fabric for all of those ideas. I've also bought fabric just because it was cool fabric, and I've bought fabric because I might need it for a project. Basically, I've become a fabric hound. At any rate, I love quilts and quilting, even though I think the Über Quilting Gene did not get passed to me. My aunt can quilt nine stitches to the inch; my grandmother could quilt ten stitches to the inch. I'm lucky if I get in six. Of course, the idea is to get as many stitches to the inch as possible.

Geena and I had met at a few quilt shows and then ran into each other at a quilt shop out in St. Charles, and finally I asked her to come and appraise the quilts that I have, which she did. Then she realized what a great little quilt shop we had in New Kassel. It's called the Fabric of Life, known as "the Fab" to us locals. I see Geena at least four times a year when the shop has its quarterly clearance sale.

Geena answered in her usual bubbly voice. "Hey, it's Torie," I said.

"Torie! How nice to hear from you," she said.

"I was wondering if you'd do me a favor," I said. "I'll pay you, of course, since it falls in the realm of your occupation."

"Got a new old quilt you want me to look at?"

"I may have several," I said. "I'm about to purchase a bunch of quilts by Glory Kendall. I need you to come down and appraise them, partly so I know what I'm getting and partly so I can pay the owner a fair price."

"Glory Kendall?" she said, instantly recognizing the name. "She's got a quilt at the Smithsonian, and her Ode to Mother won the most prestigious award at the San Francisco World's Fair in 1915. She was only seventeen when she quilted it! How have you come across such a wonderful windfall?"

"She was born and raised here in town, and the present owner of the quilts is selling them."

"Oh, that's fantastic," she said. "You're going to do right by them, I know you will. Will you have a display?"

"Oh, you betcha," I said. "Even if I don't get the Kendall house, I'll clear out a room at the Gaheimer House for them."

"The house?"

I explained to her that it was up for sale as well. "When can you come down? I think he's pretty anxious for some quick cash."

"I'm free tomorrow afternoon," she said.

"Great, I'll meet you at the Fab," I said. "I can drive you out to the house."

"Oh, I can't wait to see these quilts."

"Me, too," I said.

We said goodbye and hung up. I was about to get comfortable and watch a movie when there was a knock at the door. It was Sheriff Mort.

"Torie," Mort said, "I went by the Kendall house, and I don't see anything wrong."

"Really?" I asked.

"What's this about the Kendall house?" Rudy asked. Rudy and Mort get along really well. I think Rudy's trying to talk him into joining his bowling team. Any help Rudy's bowling team could get would be a good thing.

"Evan thinks it's haunted," I said. "I thought maybe there were squatters there."

"Oh, no," Rudy said. "That house is haunted."

I just stared at him. He plopped down in his recliner, and Matthew crawled up in his lap. Matthew was almost too big to fit there anymore, but that didn't stop him from wiggling his butt into the chair until Rudy winced. "Ouch. That's my hip, son," he said.

"What do you mean, the house is haunted?" I asked.

"Everybody knows that," Rudy said. I said nothing. Suddenly Rudy smiled. "Oh, my gosh, do I actually know something about New Kassel that you don't?"

I ignored him and turned my attention back to Mort. "No sign of breaking and entering at all?"

"No," he said, "In fact, other than some major dust, the house looked fine. I think a pipe busted a few years back, because there was a water stain on the dining room ceiling, and there's that one room on the second floor, but I saw absolutely no evidence of anybody being in the house who shouldn't be. I guess I was so set on the idea of squatters that I went right past the part about that one room.

"What's the deal with that house, anyway?" Mort asked. "It looks like a museum on the inside. Why all the furniture and stuff?"

"Well, I'm not sure," I said. "Evan bought it from Herbie Pyle back in the early eighties. Herbie had bought it from Sandy Kendall just before he died, I want to say somewhere around 1956, but I'm not sure. Since there were no surviving members of the Kendall family, when Sandy sold the house, he sold all the belongings inside as well. So most of the stuff inside probably belonged to the Kendall family. Guess I should look into that."

"Whatever," Mort said. "I found nothing wrong with the place."

"Did you check all the rooms?"

"Yeah," Mort said. "Cellar, too. Why the interest in the house?"

"I'm thinking about buying it," I said.

"We are?" Rudy asked. "When do I get to find out about this?"

"I haven't gotten to talk to you about it yet, honey," I said with a smile. "It would make a great addition to the historical society. I was concerned, of course, because if there were homeless people taking up residence in the house, there might be a lot of damage done to the property."

"No, nothing like that," Mort said.

"Wait," I said. Now my brain kicked in. "What did you say about the one room? On the second floor?"

"There were some bloodstains and stuff…"

"Bloodstains?"

"Yeah, on one of the walls."

"Probably from one of the suicides," I said.

"Oh, yeah, sounds like a house I want to buy," Rudy said.

"We can clean it up," I said.

"Clean it up?" Rudy said. "Why would I want to voluntarily clean up blood? This wasn't in the contract when I married you."

"It's blood that's almost eighty-five years old."

"Old blood, new blood, it's still blood!" Rudy said.

I sighed heavily and turned to Mort. "Thanks for checking into it for me," I said.

"No problem," he said. "But, Torie, there's some crazy stuff in that one room. The suicide room." He shook his head and then made the loony sign with his finger beside his ear. "I mean…not good."

How bad could it be? I've seen *fresh* blood from a murder scene before. Whatever was in that room at the

Kendall house couldn't be as bad as that. Nothing could ever be as bad as that.

Mort left, and Rudy's gaze followed me from the door as I walked through the living room. "Hey," he said. "I'm not cleaning up a bunch of eighty-five-year-old blood."

That's a sentence you won't find spoken in many marriages. At least I hope not.

Just then Mary walked into the house with straw in her hair and horse manure all over her shoes and pants. "I never knew horses pooped so much," she said.

"What goes in has to come out," Rudy said.

"I'll be in the shower," she said. As she walked up the stairs I heard her say, "It was just a little bit of hair spray."

I stifled a laugh, and Rudy's eyes grew huge. "I took a picture of the horses before she shampooed them," he said. "I didn't think horsehair would do that."

I laughed then, and so did Rudy. "Did anybody feed the chickens?" I asked.

"No," Rudy said.

Heading out to the chicken coop, I breathed in the intoxicating smell of an oxygen-rich night. There's something about the smell of the air in spring. The only way to describe it is green.

We don't live on a farm, but we do live on several acres just outside of town, surrounded by woods on one side, pasture on two sides, and a service road in the front. I'd brought my chickens over from the house that we used to own on River Pointe Road in town. The horses were a new addition. Already the kids wanted to buy llamas like my aunt has. I was waiting on the llamas.

We had the house built for us last year. It took me a while to get used to not being able to see Old Man River from my bedroom window. Now I look out across fields and wooded acres. I love water. I could gaze at a big body of water for hours on end and not even be aware of the time that has slipped by. Still, I have to admit, the view I have now is breathtaking.

I fed the chickens and thought about what Mort had told me. There was nothing unusual about the Kendall house, except for bloodstains in one of the rooms upstairs. No squatters. No evidence of breaking and entering or kids using the place to drink or do drugs. Was Evan Merchant crazy? Or maybe he drank a lot and hallucinated when he got drunk.

When I finished feeding the chickens, I went inside and up to my office to look up morning glories on the Internet.

THE NEW KASSEL GAZETTE
The News You Might Miss
By Eleanore Murdoch

Spring, glorious spring! It won't be long until the Strawberry Festival is upon us. But before we settle in for all those good jams and jellies, we're about ready to embark on our first—and, I've been told, annual—rose show! In honor of this new festivity, I would like to take a poll of the residents of New Kassel. Please phone in your favorite rose. That way we can get an idea of what sort of roses we should include in the show, and most likely set aside any squabble about floribundas. Call me at the Murdoch Inn with your vote!

The gnome thief is back. Unfortunately, we have been unable to catch this pervert. If anybody has any news about this, please contact our new and illustrious sheriff, Mort Joachim, at the sheriff's department in Wisteria.

Really, I thought the people of New Kassel were a more congenial lot than this. Somebody painted the spots on Elmer's dalmatian white. So now he has an all-white dog! He's not a dalmatian without spots! Father Bingham says to remind all of you that animals are God's children, too, and that whoever did this should repent.

I just received exciting news! Midwest Traveler is coming to New Kassel to do an article on our lovely town. I needn't remind everybody to keep the streets clean and be on your best behavior.

Chuck Velasco has company from out of town, so why not stop in at the pizza parlor and give them a big hello. Oh, and Lucy Kleinschmidt is looking for a new pineapple upside-down cake recipe.

Until next time,
Eleanore

FOUR

THERE WASN'T A WHOLE LOT of information on morning glories. They are found on vines, and originally they grew wild. Almost all of them only bloom in the morning. The moonflower kind only blooms at night, but I could not find a single reference to a morning glory blooming day and night. Nor could I find a single reference to a "perennial" morning glory, meaning that the flower would come back every year on its own.

I needed a flower expert.

Maybe the flower at the Kendall house wasn't a morning glory at all. Maybe Evan Merchant didn't know a morning glory from a daisy. At least that was what I told myself the next day, all the way over to Tobias Thorley's house.

Tobias lives right in the thick of "downtown." His front yard is rectangular and perfectly manicured. A mass of color graces every nook and cranny. Flowers are everywhere, and little cutesy things decorate every available space—wishing wells, fairy fountains, leprechauns, and, of course, gnomes, although the gnomes were missing at the moment. He has busts of famous people in his backyard; he has his Mozart corner and his Lincoln garden. As best I could tell, he planted whatever flower or plant represented those people to him. Tobias is much more than just the resident accordion player.

I rang his doorbell. He answered in a huff and said, "What?"

Tobias is one of those people who makes you wonder if he's actually alive or if his body is just up moving around without the benefit of heart and blood. He's old and scarecrow thin, with a hook nose and skin darkened by years in the sun. His knees are knobby, which I know because I see his knees every time he puts on his little knickers outfit for events. It's like there's nothing but skin and bones, no muscle or sinew in between.

"Hi, Tobias," I said.

"Did you steal my gnomes?"

"No," I said.

"Then I don't have time to talk to you," he said.

He started to shut the door, but I stuck my foot out to stop him. I have never been known as subtle in this town, even when I think I'm being subtle. Why start now? "Tobias, I know you want your gnomes back, but I have a really important question for you."

"It's not so much that I want my gnomes back. I can buy new ones. I just want the stealing to stop," he said. "For years, people have taken perverse pleasure in taking what's mine. I can't for the life of me figure out why anybody would want a used garden gnome!"

I started to say something, but he wasn't finished.

"No, I don't want the gnomes back, I want the cad who took them to be found and punished to the fullest extent of the law! I want...I want a public flogging!"

"Well, I doubt if you'll get a public flogging, Tobias,

because I'm not exactly sure they still do that in this country," I said. "I'm sure they'll have to go to jail or pay a fine or something, though."

"A fine," he said, and stepped outside on the front porch. "A fine? How will that make up for the years of torment and harassment that I have been put through?"

Clearly, this man was serious about his garden.

"I think I've found a morning glory that blooms all day and some nights and comes back every year," I said.

His eyes grew wide. "You don't say?" Just like that, all thoughts of those puny little gnomes went right out the window. "Can't be. No such thing. Unless it's one of those newer varieties."

"That's what I thought, too."

"Where's it at?"

"Over at the old Kendall place," I said.

"Well, let's go have a look-see." He grabbed his hat from some magical place inside his door and was off his front porch, heading for my minivan before I could even blink.

I'd deliberately waited to take Tobias to the morning glory until about one in the afternoon, so it would be after morning and he could see it blooming for himself. On the way over to the Kendall house, I asked Tobias just what was so great about gardening. I mean, my old house came with a lilac bush and maybe a few roses. I'd deliberately planted a few other things around my yard, but I'd never gone all-out with flowers and the like. At the new house, we really hadn't done much landscaping, since we'd moved in during late autumn. We should have done it this spring, but it just seemed as though there'd been too many other things to do. Plants could wait. I could almost hear Tobias gasping at my thoughts. Plants, wait?

"What's so great about gardening?" he echoed.

"Yeah," I said.

"Where to start," he said. "The smell of the earth is intoxicating, but that's not it. I could just dig a pot of dirt and keep it by my bed if that were it."

I laughed, and as I looked over at him, he winked at me.

"There is something primal, something…*real* about planting a little bitty seed and then watching it grow and grow and grow until it produces whatever it's supposed to produce: fruit, flower, tomato, whatever. The thing that drives me is a love of beauty. I can take a piece of plain old land and make it beautiful, and I made it. Plants are living things, you know. Really alive. Like people and animals. There's so many species of plants and flowers… it's relaxing, it's good exercise, it's just where I'm supposed to be."

Those were the most words I'd ever heard Tobias speak in the entire time I'd known him. Which had been my whole life. Truth be told, I hadn't known he was capable of such a speech.

I pulled into the driveway at the Kendall house, and Tobias was out of the van before I'd turned off the engine. He ran up to the wildly climbing vine—it was entangled in the porch posts and curling up along the porch ceiling— took his hat off, and scratched his head. He looked up at the sky, then fingered the leaves on the vine. Then he fingered the flowers, which were completely open and beautiful.

"Well?" I said. "Is it a morning glory?"

"Sure as hell is," he said. "It's a standard Heavenly Blue."

"What's that mean?"

"It's a type of morning glory," he said, clucking his teeth. "You say it comes back every year?"

"According to Evan Merchant."

"Well, in the tropics, that's not unheard of," he said, "but not here. Does Evan do anything special to it in the winter? Not that it matters, because this is impossible."

"No, he does nothing special. In fact, he told me that he's actually dug it up and whacked it down."

Tobias looked at me sharply.

"It just keeps coming back."

"These flowers…See, a morning glory bloom opens once in the early morning. Then it closes quickly and that bloom dies. A new one replaces it, so…And the roots, well, they're supersensitive," he said. "I can't believe it."

"So it is definitely a morning glory."

"It's a freak of nature, but yeah. And it's an oldie. This is not one of those new ones."

You know, I'd really been hoping that Tobias would tell me that Evan had been wrong about what sort of flower it was. A freak of nature…it just made me uncomfortable.

Tobias glanced over at the fence and said, "That's a wisteria bush." Then he completely digressed into what was planted where throughout the entire yard. Within ten minutes, though, he was back to studying the morning glory. He walked up onto the porch to get a better look at it from the other side. I wasn't sure what he thought a different angle would tell him, but I wasn't going to interfere with his study.

"Do you think Evan would mind if I brought the garden club over here to look at it?" he asked.

"I'm sure he wouldn't mind, especially since he's selling the house."

"Yeah, I'd heard that," Tobias said. He came down off of the porch and glanced up at the house, shading his eyes from the sun with his hat. "Well, I'm going to go and get Dudley. He's got to see this."

With that, he was off. He didn't even wait for me to give him a ride back to his house. Not that he couldn't make it to his house in ten or fifteen minutes without a ride, because he could.

My cell phone rang. The number on the screen was my mother's. "Hello?"

"Hi, it's me." Mom hasn't quite gotten used to the fact that she didn't need to identify herself on the phone anymore. With caller ID on my home phone, office phone, and cell phone, I always know who's calling unless it's somebody who doesn't want me to know. I don't answer those calls. Who would? Beyond that, she's been my mother for all the years I've been alive. Like I wouldn't recognize her voice? "I hear you're going to buy the Kendall house."

"Oh, my God, that's a record even for this town," I said.

She laughed. "Well, you know. You just have to know the right people."

"You've certainly always known the right people." My mother is in a wheelchair, has been since she was ten years old. She was one of the last children to contract polio in the early fifties before Salk's vaccine came out. That just seemed to make her all the more determined to keep me under her thumb when I was a child. I could not go anywhere in this town without her knowing it. Not then and not now. When I was about fourteen, I'd hitchhiked to

Wisteria with a friend of mine, and my mother knew about it before I'd even made it to my destination. She had the greatest network of spies I'd ever seen. Most parents subscribe to this notion of looking out for everybody's kids, but my mother had taken it to the extreme. Then again, she'd had to. It's not as if she could just get in the car and go look for me.

"I was wondering if you'd like this extra pan of vegetable lasagna that I made," she said. Did I mention my mother is one of the greatest cooks to ever grace the planet? Another great thing about my mother is that she doesn't mind sharing. She shares whatever she cooks or bakes, and she'll even share the recipe. The whole recipe. My father's mother would always leave out some special ingredient so that whatever it was would never taste quite like hers.

"Mom, why do you always ask if we want your food? You know, hands down, without a doubt, we are always gonna take your food." Not because we were poor and couldn't afford our own, but hers was just so darn good. Yes, far better than mine. You know, when I think about it, I'm not sure I inherited any of the good qualities of any of my ancestors. I'm sort of mediocre at everything.

Just then I saw Eleanore drive by, speeding ninety to nothing down the street, around the corner, and then out of town. Eleanore. Maddie. Maddie lived out of town. I needed to get over to Maddie Fulton's house before Eleanore started World War III or worse. Eleanore would catch me out in public and ask me if I'd spoken to the rogue rosarian, and if I hadn't, she was going to blow a gasket.

"When you come to get Matthew, I'll have it ready for you," she said.

"Okay, thanks, Mom."

I think cooking for us is Mom's way of trying to help me out. Rudy and I both work, and we take turns with dinner and the like. Usually, whoever gets home first starts on dinner. Most of the time it's me. So maybe this is Mom's way of trying to save my marriage. The fewer dinners of mine that Rudy has to eat, the better?

Well, at least she was subtle about it. It's not like she said, "Here's some food so your husband doesn't leave you."

I got in the van and headed toward Maddie Fulton's house. Maddie lives maybe a mile out of town, right off of the outer road. In fact, driving by her house is a treat. Tobias was right about beauty. Her yard exudes beauty, and I always take an extra long look as I drive by it. I'd just never really thought about it before.

Unlike Tobias's yard, Maddie's was not manicured or orderly. No, her yard had succumbed to flowers and blossoms and vines. I'd never seen her backyard before, so I was sort of looking forward to it. Tobias had me curious now. The house itself was a storybook house. Something you'd see in a Mary Engelbreit drawing. It was brick and had a wooden arch-shaped front door with a round window in it. Above the front door the roof came up into a point, contributing to that fairy-tale look. Even the mailbox had two different gorgeous flowering vines of some sort climbing up over it. One was white and one was purple.

Lucky for me, wherever Eleanore had been going in such a hurry, it hadn't been to Maddie's. I rang the doorbell.

Maddie answered covered in dirt, wearing an apron, mud boots, and lots of sunblock. Maddie is probably about fifty-two, with a head full of gray curls and glasses that always slide down to the very tip of her nose. She is as short as I am and always has a smile on her face. "Well, hello, Torie. Are you here about the rose show?" she asked. "I just came in to get a drink of water. I've been working all day on the roses to take. Come on in."

I entered her house, but she ushered me through it and out the back door so quickly that I barely got a chance to see what the inside looked like.

When I entered the backyard, my breath caught in my throat. Everywhere I looked were roses. There were white and yellow roses climbing all over a fence that marked one side of her yard, and they didn't just climb on the fence; they climbed up over it, hovering at least eye-level with me. Two trellises were smothered with pink roses. She even had some sort of patio cover that had orangey-colored roses climbing over the top of it, so that when you stood underneath it, the sky seemed to be made of soft, fragrant petals.

I was overwhelmed.

"Amazing, isn't it?" she asked.

"Yeah," I said.

"In case you're curious, it's called a cottage-style garden, and I do have things other than roses. So," she said with a sigh. "What can I do for you?"

"Uh…Eleanore came to see me," I said.

The smile disappeared from her face. "That woman is a plague."

"Well, maybe," I said, "but she is a respected business owner in town, and I think she means well." God, was I really sticking up for Eleanore?

"She's sent you to try to change my mind on the selections for the rose show," she said. "Am I right?"

"Dead right," I said.

"Look, Torie, I consulted with the other rosarians in town," she said. "We all came to the same agreement that too many rose shows and rose events focus on the hybrid tea. The hybrid tea has had all of its personality bred right out of it. Oh, yeah, they're great to get in a bouquet on Valentine's Day or your birthday, but I personally don't think they're the greatest roses."

"Well…"

"I have a few," she admitted. "There are some dandy specimens, and I believe every garden should have a variety, so I've picked the very best of them. Don't get me wrong, I do like them, but the rosarians in New Kassel decided it would be a really great idea to highlight some of the roses that are lesser known but just as beautiful. Roses with some heritage to them. Isn't that what this town is all about? Heritage? History? Besides, the officers of the garden club said that was perfectly fine with them. Everybody said so, except for Eleanore."

"Well…"

"Look, Torie, I know you're just trying to do your job and keep the peace and all that good stuff, but Eleanore knows nothing about roses. Oh, and now she has this ridiculous poll in the paper. Have you seen it? Urging people to call in and vote on their favorite rose. The whole point in having the garden club sponsor this show is so that people can see roses. All roses. Not just Mister Lincoln and Peace."

"Right," I said. "Well…"

"Here," she said, scooping up a handful of cuttings from the patio table. She clipped off some foliage on a few and then handed them to me. "Take these to your mother. They'll brighten her day."

That was it. I was dismissed, and I found myself following her back through her house to the front door without having even realized that I'd taken the steps.

At the last minute, something in the corner of her living room caught my eye. A beautiful appliqué quilt sat draped over the edge of an antique formal sitting chair. I knew instantly that the quilt was old, although I wasn't sure just how old. "Oh, Maddie, where'd you get that quilt?" I asked. "Can I see it?"

"Certainly," she said. "This is one of my pride and joys." She unfolded the quilt for me. It was—what else?—a floral appliqué. It looked like a dogwood, except the flower was red.

"It's a rose. *Rosa moyesii* to be exact. I see by the look on your face that you think all roses look like florists' long-stemmed red roses. The original roses were only four- or five-petaled and flat. Like *Rosa moyesii*."

"But, did you…You didn't make this quilt. It's an antique," I said.

"I know," she said. "Glory Kendall made this quilt back in the teens."

My mouth dropped open. "How did you get ahold of one of Glory Kendall's quilts?" I asked.

"I have several," she said. "A few of them are still wrapped in paper and in a plastic bag. I haven't had the chance to get them cleaned. Shoot, I think one of them still has pins in it!"

"But how?"

"My grandmother and Glory Kendall were very good friends. These were gifts to my grandmother from Glory. My grandma just passed away about four years ago. I inherited her cat, these quilts, her china, and her roses. My brother got all of the furniture. Our cousin got all of the old jewelry and her old phonograph records and the player. Wow, did my grandma ever have a collection of old records. I'm talking old seventy-eights. My mother got all sorts of things, including the family photos. I think I got the best end of the deal," she said, just as a cat that I didn't even know was there jumped down off of the recliner and scared me. "Well, except for that thing. I can't say the cat has been a blessing." She was laughing when she said it, so I got the feeling that she didn't really mean it.

"I can't believe you've got quilts by Glory Kendall," I said.

"What's your interest in them?" she asked.

"I love old quilts, and I'm thinking about starting a women's textile display at the Gaheimer House. I'm about to purchase some of Glory's quilts from Evan Merchant."

"Oh, how wonderful," she said. "Well, I have four or five of them. Let me know when you get it all together and you want to start a display. I'll loan you my grandmother's for a year or so. It's not as if I'm using them all. Of course, I do want them back, because they mean the world to me. Especially this one, since it was made specifically for my grandma. Glory knew how much my grandma loved roses."

"Oh, of course. I'm amazed you'd let them out of your sight."

"I trust you," she said. "You've always done right by this town."

I ran my fingers over the appliquéd flowers on the quilt once or twice, and then Maddie put the quilt away and I left. Once I got in the car I realized that I hadn't really accomplished much with Maddie. I'd heard what she had to say on the subject of roses for the rose show, but she hadn't heard a word I'd said. Maybe that's because I hadn't really had a chance to say anything—and I wasn't very accustomed to not getting to say much.

I really like Maddie Fulton. I always have, even though we pretty much move in different circles. Our paths do cross, however, as my path seems to cross everybody's path at some point. If you live in New Kassel and I've never met you, it's because you've stayed away from all of the town's festivals and events. Aside from that, my mother is married to the mayor—the ex-sheriff—and I also have three kids, two very active in school, so I seem to know every parent within a five-mile radius. That doesn't mean I'm good friends with all of these people. It just means that our paths cross.

After today, I thought, I might just make it a habit to drop in on Maddie once in a while. Those roses sitting on the seat next to me smelled so good that I was tempted to keep them for myself.

FIVE

GEENA CAMPBELL is in her late thirties, about five foot six, with super-dark auburn hair that reaches her shoulders. She's usually covered in little pieces of thread or fabric and wears her blue-rimmed glasses on her head more often than her nose. I think she really only uses them to hold her hair back.

I found her by the remnants bin at the Fab. When she saw me, she gave me a big old hug and immediately showed me the fantastic fabric she'd picked out and told me all about what she was going to do with it. Of course, I knew as well as she did that she wouldn't get anything done with it right away. It would go in her stash until the project that the fabric was for came to the forefront.

"You'll never guess what I found today," I said to her.

"What?"

"There's a woman here in town who has several Glory Kendall quilts," I said.

"Really," she said. "Now that's interesting."

"I have no idea why this came as such a shock to me. I mean, Glory lived here her whole life, however short it may have been, so it only makes sense that there might be townspeople who would have some of her quilts."

"Still, how odd that you'd discover this on the very day you were going to buy quilts made by the very same person," she said.

"I know."

After we talked a bit more and she paid for her fabric, I drove her out Haggeman Road to the Kendall house.

Geena stepped out of the van and put her hands on her hips. "Wow," she said. "What a great house. I mean, it could stand to have some work, but just look at that house."

"That's what I thought," I said. I started to head around back to get Evan, but he had evidently seen us pull into the driveway and was already halfway to the house. I waved to him, and when he was at the porch, I introduced him to Geena.

He seemed a bit nervous when he put the key in the keyhole. The door swung open with a creak, and he stuck his hands in his pockets. "There ya go," he said. "Let me know when you're finished."

"Wait," I said. "Evan, I have no idea where the quilts are. Aren't you going to come in to at least show me where they're kept?"

"Nope," he said. "Check in the bedroom on the second floor. The one on the far end that overlooks my house. That's not to say there aren't any others in the house, but that was her room. So I imagine that's where they're gonna be."

"But..."

"Oh, and could you pull the shade down in Glory's room, while you're up there?"

"Sure," I said.

He skipped off the front porch and disappeared around the back of the house. Geena gave me a quizzical look. "He swears the house is haunted," I explained.

"Really?" she asked with a smile.

I held my hands up. "Hey, I'm just telling you what he's told me."

She glanced back over her shoulder to where Evan had disappeared. "You're serious."

"I don't think so, but he sure does."

"Hunh. Well, let's go meet the ghosts."

We stepped inside. I flipped on the light switch, since the house was dark. It wouldn't have been quite so dark if the shades and curtains had been pulled aside to allow the sunlight in, but I assumed this was how Evan wanted the house kept, so I didn't open them. The first room we stepped into was covered in that heavy Victorian-era wallpaper and had virtually no furniture in it.

"So, explain to me about the house," Geena said.

"Well, I really don't know that much," I said. "I'm going to do some research when we get finished here today. Evan is the second owner since the Kendalls lived here. He never actually stayed in this house for very long, but instead took up residence in the guesthouse in the back. From what I understand, the majority of the things in the house belonged to the Kendalls."

We stepped down a hallway into a dining room, where cobwebs had made the crystal chandelier even more elaborate than it had started out to be. Then we moved on to another sitting-room type of room. Older houses often have rooms that we don't have uses for today, like sitting rooms and ballrooms. I guess they're the equivalent of our home-entertainment rooms. This one had clearly had some renovations done to it—new wallpaper and a new floor. "Obviously, though, Herbie Pyle, the man who lived here in between Sandy Kendall and Evan, tried to do some renovating."

"Why would that person sell the furniture and things with the house? Why not take those things with him? Or maybe sell them separately?" Geena asked.

"I have no idea," I said. "I think we're going to find what we want upstairs."

"Right," she said. She pulled two white bundles out of her blazer pocket and handed me one. "Here."

"What's this?" I said. It was a pair of white gloves, like a bridesmaid would use. "Oh, for the quilts."

"Yes," she said. "No need in getting our oils on the fabric. Makes the fabric break down faster."

"Right," I said.

The stairway seemed overly long and ostentatious, coming from the heavens and spilling into the middle of the house with a wave of dark wood. We reached the first bedroom and found a chest at the foot of the bed. Good place for quilts to be, in a chest. So we opened it and found a gold mine of antiques, including the Civil War uniforms I had heard about. "Oh, my gosh," I said. "These are amazing."

"And these?" Geena asked.

"Medals of valor of some sort," I said. "I'm afraid to move any of this stuff."

"I know," she said. So we just lifted a few of them to see if there were any quilts beneath the uniforms. There were not. There was a diary. Several diaries, to be exact. Oh, my fingers were itching to take those home and read them, but the deal with Evan was for the quilts and all things relating to them, not for the diaries. It was at moments like these that I realized I wanted to know about the who and why more than I wanted things. I'd much rather read those diaries than own those uniforms and medals.

We opened the drawers. Most of them were empty, but we did find a box of handkerchiefs that hadn't even been used and some other odds and ends. There were no closets, as was typical of some old houses. Usually closets were added later. Back then people tended to use things like wardrobes and large dressers and chests to store their things in, rather than closets.

When we opened the wardrobe, Geena exclaimed, "Eureka!" There was a pile of quilts.

"Oh, boy," I said. "You know, some of these may not have been made by Glory, but rather by her mother or any number of quilting friends or family members. How are we ever going to know which are hers?"

"Well, we can take quilts that we know for sure she made, like the ones your friend has, and compare style and stitching and fabrics that she used. She may even have initialed the ones that were hers. With some, we may never know the maker, but we might come closer than you think. For one thing, some fabrics are going to be far older than Glory."

"Yes, but couldn't she have had a stash of old fabric and used that? I have a box full of feedsack cloth from the thirties that belonged to my grandmother. If I made a quilt out of that now, who would know it wasn't an old quilt?"

"For one thing, your batting and backing would be newer and inconsistent with the wear of the other fabric," she said, "and obviously, there are going to be things about antique quilts that you'll never be able to know for sure."

Boy, I hated to hear those words. Those words drove me crazy.

"But one thing at a time," she said. "First of all, we need to catalog them. Write down the obvious things like what pattern they are, the size of the quilt…We can't do this here. It's too dark and dusty. You think Mr. Merchant will let us take them elsewhere?"

"I don't know," I said. "I mean, would you?"

"Well, Torie, you're not exactly just the average buyer. Are you purchasing these for your personal collection?"

"No," I said.

"For a museum, correct?"

"Yes."

"So where are you going to go? He knows where to find you, for crying out loud," she said.

"True," I said. "He might let us remove the quilts. Let's see how many we're dealing with for sure before I even think about asking him."

There were seven in the wardrobe in the first bedroom. The second bedroom yielded none, since it was actually more like a den. There were built-in bookshelves and an old desk; there was even a gun rack with the guns still inside. Oh, those would be worth money to a gun collector. Hanging on one wall was a rack of swords. Two were missing.

The third bedroom was so disturbing that Geena could not enter. This was the room with the blood on the wall, the room that Sheriff Mort had said had bloodstains from one of the suicides. It wasn't just the blood that was so disturbing, though. It was the mass of words and pictures scribbled all over the walls. Drawings and sketches of wounded and bleeding men had been drawn all the way up to the ceiling in some places. Men with arms and legs missing. Men lying sprawled in a trench; that one ran the length of one whole wall. The fear on their faces, the feral look in their eyes… The drawings were everywhere.

On the bedposts were old ropes or restraints of some sort.

"Oh, Jesus," I whispered.

"God, Torie, let's hurry," Geena said from the hallway. "This house is so damn dark."

"Right," I said. "I'm looking." There were no quilts in this room, but I did find a few photographs of a young woman. Beautiful, ethereal, gazing into the camera with all the innocence of a child, but the sexuality of a woman. The photographs had probably been taken about 1915. I turned one of them over. The back read: *Be brave, my one true knight. Your loving sister, Glory Anne.*

I took the photographs with me. I know it was wrong, and if Evan really wanted me to give them back, or if he wanted me to pay for them, I would, but I would need photographs to go with the quilt display. Besides…I don't know, call it my Super Torie Sense, but there was one hell of a story here. I'd been doing this a very long time, and I could feel the story in this house trying to squeeze its way to the surface for somebody, *anybody,* to hear.

If I wasn't determined at that point to get to the bottom of what had gone on in this house, the next thing that happened sealed it. The door to the bedroom had nearly shut behind me when I came in, so as I turned to leave, I got a real good look at the inside of the door. There were claw marks all over it. Somebody had locked somebody in this room, and from the looks of it had tied him or her to the bed. I could deduce—by not taking too much of a leap—that when the individual wasn't restrained, he or she had picked up a pencil and drew the nightmares in his or her head…and then at some point had bled all over the wall.

"Torie, come on!" Geena called from down the hall.

There was another bedroom, which yielded four quilts. Finally, Geena beat me to the last bedroom at the end of the hall. The one with the shades and curtains open. Glory Anne Kendall's room. Geena stood by the window, soaking up the sunlight. "This house is a tomb," she said. "And you want to buy it?"

"Well, if I buy it, I'm not going to leave it like this," I said. "For one thing, these big ugly curtains have got to go."

"I don't even want to spend another second in this house," she said.

Glory's room was bright and pink and full of finished quilts, partially finished quilts, fabric, pieces cut out but not yet sewn together, and all of her sewing equipment, including a machine. There was even a quilt still in the frame that she had clearly been in the middle of quilting.

"I can transport everything back to the Gaheimer House," I said. "I'm almost afraid to take the quilt out of the frame, though."

"No," Geena said. "We'll leave it in the frame and take it out last."

Quilting frames come in all shapes and sizes. I remember my Grandma Keith's quilt frame hung from the ceiling in her living room. It was on a pulley system. She'd pull it up to the ceiling during the day, and at night after all the other work was finished, she'd pull the string and let it down and quilt.

The three layers of a quilt—the decorative top layer, the batting, and the backing—all have to be pulled taut and then basted together with thread or pins so they won't move. Otherwise, when you go to quilt it, the layers will pucker. In order to pull them tight, you have to set them and hold them in one position, thus the frame. With a wooden frame, the quilt would be loosely basted to the pieces of wood, and then the wood could be rolled—with the quilt—as you quilted until you just had a small strip left to work on. There were lots of methods to achieve this. Nowadays, there are quilt frames made out of PVC pipe, and I even use a big embroidery hoop to quilt on my lap.

Glory had a standard wooden frame that stood on the floor. Luckily for us, it was rolled pretty tight and only had a little bit left to quilt, so it would be easy for us to transport it to the Gaheimer House. There we could put it in one of the big drawing rooms and then take it apart. Or who knows, maybe we'd just leave it as it was, so people could see what it was like to quilt back then.

"I think the easiest way to transport this is for you and me to just carry it over to the Gaheimer House. It's quite a few blocks, I know, but it's not heavy."

"All right," she said.

"Look, I made the deal with Evan for all needlework, so anything pertaining to that, we can take and pay him for."

"I found a box of her patterns in the trunk," she said. "It's not very often you actually find the patterns to go with the quilts. You've got quite a treasure here, Torie."

"Well, I want him to get every penny that they're worth," I said. "I'm not interested in making money on this, Geena. I want Glory's quilts to be seen—and I want the Kendall family story to be told."

She hugged herself close and got to work gathering quilts and notions. Suddenly she stopped, hovering over the opened chest in the corner.

"What?" I asked.

"I think it's a quilt diary," she said.

"A what?"

"It is! Oh, my gosh," she said. "Look, she has hundreds of swatches of fabric in here. Dates when and where she bought the fabric, what she would use it for…Oh, Torie, this is amazing."

It hit me then. This wonderful quilter, who spent so much time recording all of her hard work in a diary, just one day up and ended her own life. Why would she have done that? Why would any of the Kendall children have done it? Okay, well, whoever had been in the psycho room down the hall clearly had problems, but the other two? I suddenly wanted to throw up.

"Torie, look at the quilt on the bed."

It was a plain quilt. Sort of brownish, made from big blocks. Nothing fancy. Nothing fancy at all. No appliqué, no frillies, no flowers, no clever interlocked pieces. Just big brownish squares. "Why would a woman who could create absolute art with a needle choose to put that on her bed?" Geena asked.

"I don't know," I said.

"I need air," she said. With that, Geena grabbed a stack of quilts and ran out of the room and down the stairs.

I gathered up the remaining quilts and all of the other things that I wanted to take and met her out on the front porch, but not before I pulled the shade on Glory's window as Evan had asked.

I found Geena standing by the morning glory, clutching the quilt diary to her chest. "We have to find out what happened to her," she said.

"I know," I said.

"You can do that, can't you? I mean, this is what you do best, right?"

"Well, I try," I said.

"Then you have to try," she said.

"I intend to," I said.

I ran around back and asked Evan if it was okay if we took the quilts somewhere else for Geena to appraise them, since it would be hard for her to work in the dark and dusty environment. He agreed without much argument. We drove the first load over to the Gaheimer House and then came back to the Kendall house to get the quilt that was still in the frame.

As Geena and I carried the quilt out into the sunlight, I got a good look at the design. I gasped and dropped my end of the quilt frame. "What?" Geena asked.

The quilt Glory had been working on when she killed herself was an appliqué floral design. A purplish blue morning glory.

"N-nothing. I stepped in a hole," I said. I picked up the frame and made sure that I hadn't broken it. It was still in perfect condition. "Can't believe I just dropped an antique."

"Well, at least it wasn't china," Geena said. "You'd be screwed for sure if it had been china."

"Right," I said. We headed to the van. I had decided to take the seats out of the back of the van, so we could try getting the frame in, and was surprised to find that it almost fit. I tied a little red flag to the part that was sticking out. We were only going a few blocks anyway.

As I pulled out of the driveway, I couldn't help but take a long look at the morning glory vine growing up the side of the porch. Coincidence. Had to be.

SIX

GEENA AND I SPENT THE REST of the day cataloging the quilts. We searched each quilt for initials or dates. Nine of the twenty-one finished quilts had GAK quilted somewhere on them, usually in the lower right-hand corner, so we knew for certain those nine were Glory's. We could assume the quilt in the frame was Glory's, and the partially completed quilts as well. In Glory's cedar chest were no fewer than eleven finished quilt tops. The quilt tops were just that, only the top layer. They were waiting to be quilted and hemmed. I had to smile at this, because it always took me much longer to quilt a quilt than to piece one together. In fact, I had four finished tops waiting in a plastic storage bin for me to quilt. I'm not sure why, but this made me feel a bit closer to this girl who had lived a hundred years ago. I guess it was because some things are universal, and even nearly a hundred years ago, this girl suffered from the same thing I did. So much to do, so little time.

Aside from determining which quilts were Glory's, we also separated them into types: pieced, whole cloth, appliqué, etc. We might never determine who made the other twelve quilts—the ones without Glory's initials—but we at least needed to determine their approximate age.

We worked until almost sunset. Finally, Geena stretched

and winced at a pain in her lower back. "I need to call it a day," she said. "Can I come back tomorrow?"

"Of course you can come back tomorrow," I said. "I'll be here bright and early. My sister is working tomorrow, too, so somebody will be here when you arrive."

She paused at the front door and turned to me. "I don't know what happened to that girl—or what happened in that house—but at least her quilts will finally be seen."

"Yeah," I said.

"Torie, have you seen the craftsmanship in those quilts?"

"Yes," I said.

"She was amazing."

"I know," I said.

Geena left me alone to ponder the day. I walked back to my office and called Rudy. I asked him to pick up Matthew from my mother's because I was going to be a little late. I wanted to do some research on the Kendall family suicides. I knew Sylvia probably had a file on the family. Hell, Sylvia probably had known Glory Kendall. In fact, they would have been born right about the same time, within five years or so of each other.

Right now, though, I wanted to do my own research. One thing I'd learned about Sylvia was that she often tainted her research with her own prejudices. Ironic, considering the woman was all business and no pleasure, most of the time. She rarely let her personal life interfere—in anything. Be that as it may, I had seen her more than once make a mental leap based on her opinion of whatever family she was researching, so I thought it would be better if I dug a little on my own and then later read whatever Sylvia had on the Kendalls. As of right now, I really didn't know any more about the family than most other people in New Kassel did. Besides, I wanted the documents to tell me the story, not somebody else.

The first thing I did was head over to Santa Lucia, the Catholic church. By the time I reached the church, it was nearly six in the evening. The sun was getting lower in the sky, but I still had a while before it set. The church is made of stone and has Gothic-arched stained-glass windows along two sides. It really is a very pretty church, and the only Catholic church within twenty miles.

I'd noticed a rosary among some of the things in Glory's cedar chest, so, unless it had been someone else's, she was most likely Catholic. I had checked the cemetery records at the historical society before I left. The members of the historical society and volunteers had spent long hours cataloging every tombstone in every cemetery in Granite County and putting the records in book format for the historical society library. Sure enough, Glory Anne Kendall was buried in the Santa Lucia cemetery. Right next to her parents. However, her two brothers were not. The date on her death was recorded as June 14, 1922. Her father had lived to 1956. Her mother, of course, had preceded all the children in death, having died in 1913.

So where were her brothers buried?

I walked quickly through the cemetery until I found Sandy Kendall's tombstone. It was huge, about five feet tall and made of very stately white marble. His wife's stone, to his left, was a smaller version of it. Both paled seriously in comparison to Glory's. When I realized that this was the grave of Glory Kendall, I felt like an idiot. How many times had I seen this monument and even commented about how gorgeous it was, never realizing it belonged to the young woman who had killed herself on Haggeman Road?

Lounging on top of a marble tomb that must have been four feet high was a full-sized sculpture of Glory Kendall, lying on her side, raised up on one elbow, her hand cradling her face; the other hand lay gently on her hip. It was both beautiful and creepy all at the same time. The tomb was engraved with the words: *Glory Anne Kendall. Beloved daughter, angel of God, sleep forever in the arms of the Lord. Entered this world the 2nd of April 1897. Ripped from our hearts the 14th of June 1922.*

She'd been a whopping twenty-five years old. I suppose, back then, her father was most likely worried that she'd be a spinster. Nowadays, girls were just finishing up college about that age. I headed back toward the church, glancing over my shoulder at Glory Kendall's likeness.

I knocked on the rectory door, and Father Bingham answered. I've noticed that at the bigger churches in the city or even in St. Louis County, not too many priests answer their own doors. Usually a secretary or a house-keeper does that. Father Bingham almost always answers his own door unless he's saying mass or hearing confession. What hair he has left is dark, like his beard, and behind his glasses his eyes are very kind. He isn't over-weight by any means, but you definitely get the feeling that he doesn't miss any meals.

"Torie," he said. "How can I help you?"

"I was wondering if I could look at the records," I said.

"What are you interested in?" he said, as he motioned me into his home. There was a photograph of the new pope in the hallway, but I saw that Father Bingham had just moved Pope John Paul II's photograph to the other wall. He noticed me looking. "Can't imagine this hallway without John Paul."

"Oh," I said.

"So what are you looking for?" he asked.

"I want to do some research on the Kendall family," I said. "In fact, I was wondering where the sons were buried. They're not in the cemetery with Glory and her parents."

Father Bingham shook his head. "You know, back then…they probably wouldn't have allowed them to be buried here. Since they committed suicide."

"Well, yes, but so did Glory Kendall."

"I'm not sure why, but Sandy Kendall got special dispensation to get Glory buried next to him," he said. "Father O'Brien never disclosed the reasons to me before he retired. Only that Sandy had gotten special dispensation."

"Oh," I said. My mind was racing. What special dispensation? What would be the grounds for a dispensation to get a suicide victim buried in sacred ground?

"You know, so many things have changed now," he said. "Thanks to Vatican II."

"Right," I said.

"There was a man who showed up to church every day, best Catholic I'd ever seen, but when he died his wife had him put in a Protestant cemetery. When I asked her why, she said it was because he'd never divorced his first wife. He'd simply picked up and moved to Missouri, where she'd met him. He told her the truth, and she agreed to go along with the charade, but when it came time to bury him, she couldn't lie anymore. She felt compelled. So he's buried out at the Methodist cemetery. Honestly, though, since the Second Vatican Council, he could probably have been buried here and nobody would have said anything to her. Some of the older people can't get used to the new way of doing things. I had one old lady just last month ask if we were ever going to have a Latin mass again." He chuckled at the thought of it.

"You don't have to tell me weird burial stories. My great-grandfather put tombstones in a churchyard for two of his children that weren't even buried there. They were buried ten miles away in the Baptist cemetery. Seems these two children had died, he'd ordered the tombstones, and then while he was waiting for the tombstones to arrive, he got into a big fight with the minister at the church and said he'd never set foot on that church soil again. And he didn't. When the tombstones came in, he put them in the Method-ist cemetery, which was the new church that he was attend-ing. So there are two unmarked graves at the Baptist cemetery, and two stones without bodies at the Methodist cemetery. All because my great-grandfather was stubborn. Guess he didn't learn too much in Sunday school about for-giveness, huh?"

Father Bingham laughed at my story. "You always have the most interesting tales to tell," he said.

I shrugged and smiled. "At any rate, I was wondering if I could get some dates from the records, so then I could go to the newspapers and look for articles."

"Sure," he said. He led me into an office where all of the church records are kept on shelves lining the walls. It's a room that I've been in many times.

"What do you know about the Kendall family?" I asked just as he was about to leave me to the books. Father

Bingham is about sixty now, maybe a little younger, so it's not as if he was around when the Kendall suicides happened. Still, being a man of the cloth, he might have heard a good number of stories about the family.

"Not much," he said, "but when you're finished here, I might have a few names of people who would know something. One man lives over in Wisteria. He puts flowers on Glory's grave every June. He must be ninety. I have no idea what his connection is to her or the family, but I know his name."

"All right," I said. "I'll get that from you when I'm finished."

He left me to my business, and at first all I could do was stare at the walls. I have no idea why, but suddenly I felt overwhelmed, as if there were a huge and daunting task ahead of me. I took a deep breath and pulled a book from one of the shelves.

It was the baptismal records for the 1890s. Glory was born in 1897, so I assumed her brothers weren't too much older or younger than she was. For some reason I felt that Glory was the baby of the family. Just a hunch? Maybe it was some tidbit of town gossip that I'd picked up down through the years and didn't even realize it. The baptismal records revealed that, indeed, she was the youngest. Well, except for a sister who had died at three months of age, who had been born in 1900. Glory's brothers were Whalen Sanders Kendall, born in 1891, and Rupert Anthony Kendall, born in 1894. The great thing about parish records is, as long as you were a member of the parish, sometimes other notes would be added to your baptismal records. Some of my ancestors from France, for instance, have who they married and when they died penciled in next to their baptismal records.

Next to Whalen and Rupert Kendall were their death notes. Nothing extravagant, just the years 1922 and 1921. So within twelve months Sandy Kendall lost all three children to suicide. What the hell had happened? It was fairly rare for a suicide to happen in any family, but three? Within a year? And all three just happened to be siblings? Well, at least I knew which newspapers to check, which was what I had come for.

As I left the room, Father Bingham was coming around the corner with a cup of hot tea. "Do you want some?" he asked.

"No, thanks," I said. "I've got to get going."

"Find what you wanted?"

"Sort of," I said. "What I really want is to know what happened to that family, and the baptismal records can't tell me that."

"Marty Tarullo," he said. "That's the old guy's name. Lives in Wisteria on…oh, can't remember."

"That's all right," I said. "I can get his address from the white pages, either online or the old fashioned way."

"The only other person that I know of who might be able to help you is a woman named…um…Judy Pipkin."

"Oh, I know Judy Pipkin," I said. "She's done some volunteer work for the historical society. Why would she be able to help?"

"She has some connection to the family. I'm not sure what it is."

"Wow. Well, thanks for the tips," I said.

"You're welcome," he said. "Let me walk you out."

"No, that's all right," I said. "I know my way."

I left Father Bingham drinking his tea in the study.

I walked back over to the cemetery to take another look at the marble statue of Glory. The statue was intoxicating, breathtaking and pitiful all in one. It was difficult not to look at it. It was so real and lifelike that I would swear she could just swing her legs over the tomb and jump down. If she did, of course, I'd pass out right then and there.

Glory's mother's name was Hannah. On the other side of Hannah Kendall's grave was a small but sweet stone for the baby girl who had died at three months. Apparently the whole family was here. Except for the two boys.

Instead of going home, I went back to the Gaheimer House to look again at the compiled cemetery records for Granite County. I couldn't stand not knowing where Whalen and Rupert Kendall were buried. It didn't matter. Knowing where they were buried was not going to help me know what happened in that house, or why three perfectly healthy twenty-something American kids killed themselves. I just had to know. The cemetery records showed that Whalen and Rupert were buried right next to each other in the Methodist cemetery about a mile or two outside of town on the south road.

Well, at least I knew now. I grabbed Glory's quilt journal to take home and look through tonight, turned the lights off, and locked up. I had just stepped out onto the sidewalk when my stepfather drove by. I waved and he honked. Then he backed up and stopped in front of the Gaheimer House. Only in a town this size can you just back up on the main street and not hit anybody.

"Hey," I said.

He got out of the car, but stood in its open door. I guess he did that so he could jump back in and move the car, in case somebody drove by and wanted to use that side of the road. Colin is about twelve years older than I am and has earned the nickname Bubba. He's the biggest guy I think I've ever met personally with the exception of a character named Tiny Tim Julep. Colin is immensely tall, with huge hands and wide shoulders. His size somehow emphasizes the fact that he always looks ticked off. At least, when he's around me he always looks ticked off. Either way, he and my mother make quite a cute couple, since my mother is only about four foot ten, dainty, and fair. Me? I look like my dad. Put a dress on my dad, a few more eyelashes, and a slightly more feminine mouth, and you'd have me.

"Whatcha up to?" Colin asked. "You're here late."

"Oh, nothing," I said. "Just some research."

"I could see the look on your face as I drove by. Even in the dark."

"What look?" I said.

"You've got that preoccupied look."

"So? A person's not allowed to be preoccupied?" I asked.

"Come on. What is it? Who turned up mysteriously dead?"

"Nobody," I said, giving a slight shrug.

"Did you find Jimmy Hoffa this time?"

"Jeez, Colin, you need a life."

"I have a life," he said. "I am mayor of New Kassel."

"Yeah, just keep saying that to yourself. Makes you sound important."

"Torie…" He looked off up the street.

"You're bored to death, aren't you?" I asked.

"I've never played so much golf in my life," he admitted.

"Well, you asked for this job."

"It's not as if there isn't some work to do, because there is," he said. "It's just not…"

"Exciting?" I asked. "Pushing a pencil doesn't get your blood pumping?"

"Well, for all intents and purposes, being sheriff of the Middle of Nowhere, Missouri, shouldn't get my blood pumping, either. You know, the occasional speeding ticket or drug bust…"

"I've managed to keep quite busy without dealing with speeding tickets or drug busts," I said.

"That's because you're not satisfied with the crime of this century, you've got to go digging it up from the past," he said.

"At least I'm not bored and getting skin cancer from playing too much golf."

He shrugged, smiling. "The upside is that my golf game has really improved."

"Well, good, Colin. I'm happy for ya," I said. "I need to get home now. I probably missed dinner as it is."

"Whatcha working on? Come on, Torie, tell me. Please?"

I laughed. "I'm looking into the Kendall suicides."

"I knew it!" he said, and slapped the roof of his car. "You had that look!"

"Great, okay, I'm going home now."

"All right," he said. "I'll see you later."

With that he drove off. I laughed at him all the way to my car.

SEVEN

MATTHEW NEARLY KNOCKED me over when I walked through the door. He gave me a big hug and then showed me a very purple smudge under his left eye. "I got a black eye," he said.

"I see that. What happened?"

"Your daughter gave it to him," Rudy said, coming in from the kitchen.

"My daughter?" I asked. Funny how that works. An immaculate conception took place and I knew nothing about it. Hmm…I guess that is the way it would work, isn't it? I wouldn't know there was an immaculate conception taking place until after it was over. "How did she give him a black eye?"

You'll notice I didn't ask *which* daughter gave him the black eye. There was absolutely no need.

"Mary was hanging him off of the back fence by his ankles."

I couldn't help it, I laughed. Oh, come on. You can only be angry so much. Sometimes you just have to laugh at things. "Why was she hanging him by his ankles?"

"I asked her to!" Matthew said.

"Evidently he weighed more than Mary realized and she dropped him. Right on his head. On a rock," Rudy said.

I ruffled Matthew's hair. "Well, I can't say that I feel

sorry for you, buddy. If you ask your sister to hang you by your ankles, bad things are certain to follow."

"I was trying to fly," he said.

I laughed even harder. "Well, you crash landed."

The look in his eyes told me that his mind was quickly flashing through other possible ways to fly. Ones that might be more successful. Something told me this wouldn't be his only black eye.

Rudy kissed me on the cheek. "You missed dinner."

"I thought I might."

"It's still warm, though. We just finished."

"Great," I said.

I walked into the kitchen, where the smell of my mother's lasagna was still heavy in the air. I made myself a plate and ate leaning up against the kitchen counter.

Mary ran into the kitchen, yanked open the refrigerator, and pulled out a container of yogurt. "Didn't you just eat?" I asked.

"I'm hungry," she said. She grabbed a spoon and ran back out of the kitchen.

I ate in silence for a while. Then Rudy came and stood next to me. "What's up?" he asked.

"Nothing," I said. "This lasagna is good."

"Wish I could take credit for it," he said.

Rachel and Mary raced into the kitchen as the phone rang. "I got it!" Rachel yelled. Mary tried to grab the phone at the last second and Rachel accidentally elbowed her in the chest. As Mary jumped back, she hit one of the chairs and knocked it over. At least she managed not to spill any of the yogurt she was still holding.

"Is it for me?" Mary asked, recovering her dignity.

Rachel looked at the caller ID. "No! Oh yeah, it's for me this time!" Then she stuck her tongue out at Mary and disappeared with the cordless phone.

"You know, I've been thinking," I said.

"About putting the kids up for adoption?" Rudy asked.

I smacked his arm. He just laughed.

"No, I'm being serious," I said.

"Oh, in that case. Uh-oh."

"No, really. Look at our kids. We have three kids. Just like the Kendalls had. I can't imagine that our three kids would off themselves. I mean, they might end up killing each other, but I just don't see them killing themselves."

"What the hell are you talking about?" he asked, lost.

"You know, the Kendall family. The triple suicides."

"Oh, last century. Gotcha."

"How does something like that happen, Rudy? I mean, their poor father. Can you imagine? It would be devastating enough for that to happen to one of them, but all three of them? I mean…where did it go wrong? I imagine they had moments in their home like the ones we have. Playful moments, loving moments, fighting moments."

"We have loving moments? And I missed them?"

I punched his arm this time. "You know we do."

"I don't know, Torie," he said, rubbing his arm. "All I know about the Kendall family is that everything went wrong when the one brother came back from World War I. He was never the same. That's the legend circulating around town."

"So, what, let's say you have a brother, Rudy. He comes back from Desert Storm or the Iraq war and he's a bit touched. He's not quite 'right' anymore. Posttraumatic stress disorder, or whatever you want to call it. What are the chances that you and your sister would commit suicide because your brother had a hellacious war experience? I mean, does that make any sense? I can understand the veteran coming back and being unable to live with the things he witnessed, or even did, but what caused the sister and the other brother to kill themselves, too?"

"Maybe it was some bizarre death pact," he said. "I've heard of groups of friends doing that."

"True," I said, "but usually when that happens they all do it on the same day. I know at least one of the Kendall children died almost a year after the other two. I can't make it right in my head, Rudy. I just can't."

"So I take it you're going to be absent until you figure it out."

"Huh?"

"Well, physically you'll be here, but mentally you're going to be off somewhere else."

"Yeah, probably."

"All right, just as long as I know up front what I'm dealing with," he said, smiling. God bless him. "Has Mort asked you to look into this?"

"No," I said. "This is strictly on my own. There's no reason for Mort to ask me to look into it. I really just want to know what happened, so that when I do get the display of Glory's quilts up and running, I can tell her story. The whole story."

"Betcha Colin's glad he's not sheriff anymore," he said.

"Betcha he's not," I said. I set my plate in the sink and then kissed Rudy on the mouth. "I'll do homework duty if you do cleanup."

"Deal," he said.

"Oh, and by the way, can I buy the Kendall house?" I asked.

"I was wondering when you were going to get around to that," he said.

"Well, since my inheritance from Sylvia, it's not as if we can't afford it," I said. "Although I'm not sure what Evan is asking for it yet."

"What are you going to do with it?" he asked.

"I've been thinking I'd like to set it up as a textile depository. You know, not just for New Kassel. I could make it a depository of quilts and fabric arts—historic in nature—for several counties. I could do a display of Glory's work at the Gaheimer House if I had to, but I think it would be better if it's displayed in her home, and then we can display other antique textile arts there as well. When people come to see the antique textiles, they also get the history of the Kendall family. Whatever that may be."

Rudy smiled at me.

"I think it's really important, Rudy. I mean, men get giant museums and such to show off their military prowess. Hell, they get entire battlefields to show how well they can kill each other. I think women are entitled to a museum dedicated to their textile arts."

"It's fine with me," he said. "As you said, we can afford it. Although, are you sure you have a staff big enough to cover both the Gaheimer House and the Kendall house?"

"If I have to hire somebody part-time for one house or the other, I will. Besides, I might be able to get somebody like Geena to come and work one day a week at the Kendall house. I might try to get a few experts on staff. Especially if we continued to acquire more textiles."

"I think it's a brilliant idea," he said.

"Great," I said with a big smile. "I'll call our real estate agent first thing in the morning." Mission accomplished, I turned to head up to my office.

Rudy stopped me. "Do you need me for the rose show?"

"Oh, uh…you might want to run one of the refreshment booths. Otherwise, I think Tobias and Elmer have everything else covered."

"Okay," he said.

"You might want to call Colin. I think he's bored."

Rudy laughed. "I'll see him tomorrow night. Bowling."

"Ah," I said. With that I went up to my office and put Glory's quilt journal on my desk. Then I changed clothes and headed back downstairs to help with the multiple rounds of homework.

WHEN I WAS FINISHED helping Matthew write his numbers and letters and fumbling through Mary's math homework, I headed back upstairs to my office and the quilt journal. The pages of the diary were yellowed, the ink a sepia brown, faded from their original colors. I flipped through the diary just to see what was inside. It wasn't all words. There were fabric swatches with notes telling the origin of the fabrics and which quilts she had used them in. There were a few photographs tucked inside the journal, too. One photograph was of a young man sitting on the front porch of the Kendall house. There was no morning glory vine in the photograph, but there was a quilt. The quilt was wrapped around the young man, who looked pale and shellshocked. I flipped the photograph over. Written on the back was *Rupert, 1919.*

So that was brother number two. I was going to go way out on a limb here, but I'd say that he was the one who had fought in the First World War. I could find the answer to that quickly enough, since the St. Louis County public library had all of the Missouri draft papers from World War I on file. Getting his military records from the National Archives wouldn't be that difficult, either, even without his regiment information. The problem was that it could take up to eight weeks. At least that was how long it took the last time I'd sent off to the National Archives for something.

There were a few other photographs. One showed two of Glory's quilts hanging out on the laundry line. She stood demurely between them, hands folded and eyes half hidden underneath a big old flowery hat.

The journal itself began around 1913, when she was sixteen years old. She boldly stated right off the bat that she had made her very first quilt when she was just eight years old. Before that, she had helped her mother out by cutting fabric and even stitching on quilts; her mother turned her loose in the fall of 1905 to make one for her own bed. In the journal she bemoaned the fact that she had no "color swatches" from those first quilts to include.

At sixteen she was cheery, frank, and opinionated. Not unlike Rachel, only I think Glory might have been a bit more cheery. The first quilt that she journaled was a Lone Star made of red and yellow calicos. It took me only a matter of minutes to realize that Geena and I had uncovered merely a fraction of Glory's quilts. From the ages of eight to sixteen, before the start of the journal, she claimed to have made fifteen quilts. That was nearly two quilts a year. As the journal wore on, she became more prolific with patchwork quilts. By the time she was twenty, she was making about three patchwork quilts a year, plus one appliqué quilt that would take as long as the three patchwork quilts put together. Well, I could certainly relate to that. Appliqué is hard. At least I think so. Turning those edges under is as tedious as coloring my hair, strand by strand.

I was delighted to see that when she made quilts as gifts, she noted who the recipient was. Geena and I might be able to track these quilts down—if they still existed—and purchase them for the textile museum. Or possibly, if an owner was unwilling to part with a quilt, we could get it on loan, at least for the initial opening of the display. If nothing else, we could get photographs of them. It could take years to track them all down, I told myself, but it was doable.

Around 1917 Glory began to quilt even faster. It was her entire world. In that year alone, she made six quilts. Considering some quilts could have as many as a thousand pieces, all traced, cut out, and then sewn together, that was a lot—not to mention the time that went into quilting the three layers together. The reason for her speed-quilting was simple: Her brother went off to war in France. Whether she was aware of it or not, quilting became therapy. It was the only thing that got her through her brother's absence. In her words, *My beloved Rupert is deep in the trenches of France. I am so fraught with worry I can barely sleep. The only solace I find is in the stitches of my quilts.*

From 1917 to 1920, she made twenty quilts.

At some point in 1920 her quilting came to an abrupt end for nearly two years. The last quilt she made before this hiatus was a utilitarian brown one composed of big square blocks from her brother's army uniform. The entry read, *I shall make no beauty in a world so ugly. Until my brother regains his love of life, I shall sleep beneath his uniforms. Until then, I am afraid that I, too, am stricken with his sickness. The sickness of being alive in a world that cares not for life, but only for death.*

Well, that, rather melodramatically, answered the question of the plain brown quilt on her bed.

For the next year or two she chronicled the quilts she had in her possession that had been made by her mother. It seemed that only three of her mother's quilts survived. Then she documented a quilt made by her Grandmother Kendall, and there was even a quilt made by her mother's grandmother. I made notes of all of these in a notebook to give to Geena. Tomorrow she could take these descriptions and see if any of the quilts were among the ones that we had retrieved from the Kendall house.

Somewhere around Christmas of 1921, for an unknown reason, Glory picked up her needle and started to quilt again. The first quilt she made was a rose appliqué that she made for her best friend, Elspeth Bauer. I wrote this name down as well, because I was almost certain this was Maddie Fulton's grandmother. I would ask her tomorrow.

Glory finished the rose appliqué and then started on a morning glory, which was clearly the quilt that Geena and I found still in the frame in her room. Glory gave no reason for why she began quilting again. Maybe her brother got better. Maybe she got better and he didn't. At any rate, her journal entries were not chipper and bright like they had been when she was sixteen. Rather, they were fairly sedate and purposeful. There were several references to things like *not having the energy to write my name, much less sit up and quilt.* One entry in particular really bothered me. *When I am gone, I realize that there will be nothing to show I was ever here, except my quilts. I shall never be Missus Anybody. I shall never be a mother. I shall never change the world with great acts of humanitarianism. All there will be is what my fingers have produced.*

This entry was from around May of 1922. She was dead a month later.

So maybe the reason she began quilting again was to leave a record of her life. But then, why end it when she was in the middle of creating one of her most gorgeous pieces?

Her death made absolutely no sense.

EIGHT

"WELL, OF COURSE HER DEATH makes no sense," Father Bingham said from behind his desk at the rectory.

Rudy is what they call a "cradle Catholic," but I am not. Somehow I had taken to divulging my problems to Father Bingham anyway, like some sort of regular therapy session. Maybe it was because, in this town, I felt as though I couldn't say just anything to people. My best friend, Collette, had moved to Arizona, and although I had friends like Helen and others, I couldn't just dump on them about people and problems within their own town. My mother was a good listener, but being married to the mayor, who at one point had been sheriff, sort of gave her a conflict of interest. I could still go to my mother with all sorts of things, but now there were some categories of problems that I no longer felt I could discuss with her.

Enter Father Bingham.

"So, you agree?" I asked.

"Suicide never makes sense," he said.

"It must make sense to some people, or they wouldn't do it."

"At the time they are committing the act, they've convinced themselves that there is no way out," he said. "They've convinced themselves that their problems are so huge, their pain so great, that there is no other answer.

Almost always, a year later or five years later, whatever their problem was works itself out. Of course, they'll never know that."

"Yes, but…"

"You can't make sense of something that you've never experienced," he said. "It's sort of how we, as Westerners, can't understand how Muslim women can tolerate their position in their society. We say things like, 'Can't they see they're being manipulated and bullied?' But they don't see it that way. They look at you in your jeans and T-shirt and think that you're out walking around half-naked and shameful. Neither one of you can fully understand the other's feelings because you've never been in the other's place. It's foreign to you. Suicide is foreign to you, unless you've attempted it or contemplated it yourself."

"But why?"

Father Bingham took a long draw on his pipe and then tapped it on his ashtray. It was an action that I had watched my Grandpa Keith do a thousand times. Maybe that's why I connect to Father Bingham. He reminds me of my grandpa.

"Some people commit suicide because they are truly depressed. They have a chemical imbalance in the brain. According to your research, Glory speaks of not having the energy to get out of bed. Depression does that to some people. Saps them of all their energy. They stop doing the things they love, like, in Glory's case, quilting."

"Ah, but she gave a reason for that," I said.

"Nevertheless. Some people end their lives because they can't face their loved ones with something they've done. Quite often, it's nothing more than ego. They can't face people. Sometimes they can't live with an unspeakable act. Some people just see no hope for the future. Sometimes they are so mentally ill that they are in pain every single day of their lives. Sometimes they commit suicide out of anger. I actually knew a young man who took his own life as revenge against his father. He knew the thing that would bother his father most was for him to die. The ridiculous thing is, then he wasn't around to enjoy his success in hurting his father."

I shook my head. "So what do you think happened to the Kendall family?"

"I told you yesterday that I don't have a clue, but I think there was a lot of pain in that house. Just from things that townspeople have said."

I thought of the drawings in Rupert's room—and the restraints.

"What about posttraumatic stress disorder?" I asked. "I think Rupert Kendall was suffering from it. Could his illness somehow have infected the rest of the family?"

"What, you mean his attitude somehow rubbed off on them?"

"Yeah," I said.

"Well, I'm no expert, but I do think if you had to live with somebody who was suffering from PTSD, especially at a time when it really wasn't understood, it would be very difficult to accommodate. I imagine Glory probably had to take care of her brother, since her mother had already died. What must that have been like for her? She must have witnessed some pretty scary and ugly things coming from him, if he was truly suffering from PTSD. I could see how that would depress her."

I said nothing.

"Are you certain he had PTSD?"

"Oh…," I said, remembering those stricken faces sketched on Rupert's walls, "I'm pretty sure."

"Without the proper medical attention…Well, imagine a young girl having to deal with that on a daily basis? It probably did wear at her. Probably ground her down to just a shell," he said.

"So you think that Rupert's disorder affected Glory so much that she became depressed enough to kill herself?"

"I am no expert," he said. "I'm just saying that I could see how that situation would be difficult. Especially back then. With no medical or outside help. It would have all fallen to Glory, most likely. I think it would have made her doubt everything. Especially if she loved her brother. What must that have been like, for a sheltered girl to suddenly see a brother she loves in such mental anguish?"

"Right," I said. "In a world that didn't respect life, but only death."

"What?" he asked.

"Something she wrote in her quilt journal," I said.

"You have a journal of hers?" he asked. "Doesn't that give you some clues?"

"Well, it's not exactly a diary. It's something she journaled her quilts in, so she only gives hints of what was going on. She was clearly devoted to him, and she was greatly affected by his disorder. I can tell that much from the diary."

He made a gesture with his hands as if that explained it all.

"But she was equally devoted to her craft. I just can't make it right. Not that she wouldn't end her own life, but that she would do it before she finished her last quilt. That seems completely out of character for her."

"Maybe it all became too much," Father Bingham said.

"Or," I said, suddenly sitting up straight, "maybe Rupert had killed himself first, and she couldn't bear to go on. Unfinished quilt or not."

Father Bingham nodded in my direction, agreeing to what I said.

"I've got to get to a library and find some newspapers," I said. "I'll bet you anything, Rupert killed himself first, and Glory couldn't take it. That would make sense."

Father Bingham smiled at me. "Sometimes there are no pat answers," he said. "There are some things that you'll never make right."

"Yeah, but not for lack of trying," I said, and stood. "Thanks, Father."

I called the Gaheimer House on the way out of the rectory. My sister, Stephanie, answered the phone on the second ring. "Steph, it's me, Torie."

Stephanie is my younger half sister, and I only just discovered she existed a few years back. When I met her she was a history teacher, but she had since quit her job and come to work for me part-time. It gave her more time to be with her new baby and her daughter. We are a lot alike, which lends credence to that whole biology-over-environment thing. We don't look too much alike, but we do have the same eyes. In fact, it had been her eyes that convinced me she was telling me the truth when she showed up in my office, claiming to be my sister. I had, of course, been in denial—especially when I'd discovered that my father had known about her for years, had even gone to see her, and had never told me—but when I got over the hurt, I gained a fantastic addition to my family. In fact, I liked having a sister so much that I had jokingly asked my father if there were any more half siblings wandering around that I could rein in. He had muttered something about me being a brat, and no, there were no others.

"Hey, Torie, when are you coming in?" she asked.

"Not for another couple of hours. I'm headed over to Wisteria to look up something in the Granite County newspapers," I said. "I just wanted to give you a heads-up that a woman named Geena Campbell would be coming by."

"What for?" she asked. "And what are all these quilts in the front room?"

"That's why she's coming," I said. "She's an appraiser and a quilt historian. Just give her whatever she needs. Call my cell phone if she's got any questions."

"All right," she said. "I'll talk to you when you get here."

As I drove out to Wisteria, I dialed my real estate agent and told her I wanted to make an offer on the Kendall house. She said she would get back to me with specifications of the asking price and so forth. I couldn't let that house go to anybody else, particularly Eleanore. For one thing, I wanted a World War I historian to photograph and document Rupert's room.

Wisteria is the largest town in Granite County, which isn't saying much. The population has grown considerably over the past few years, and it's now around twenty thousand people. Main Street through town should be renamed Fast Food Alley, as every fast-food chain in the Midwest seems to be represented here.

There's no point in going all the way up to the St. Louis

County library when the Wisteria library holds the Granite
County newspapers. The librarians know me here. In fact,
I'd say every librarian within a sixty-mile radius knows
who I am. Today's librarian, a small blonde named Hilary,
waved at me as I came in and nodded when I signed in to
use the microfilm reader.

Once I was set up on a microfilm reader, I flipped
through the pages until I came to the article about Glory.
I had looked her up first, because I knew the exact date of
her death, whereas I only knew the year that Rupert had
died. It would save time.

Not only did Glory Anne Kendall's suicide make the
front page—it was a small community, after all—but the
paper had a photograph of her as well. I put money in the
reader and made copies of the article, but I read it sitting
there anyway. According to the paper, Glory had taken a
large dose of laudanum to kill herself. Her father gave a
statement claiming that since her brother's suicide she had
been melancholy and took no joy in life. The paper said
that Rupert Kendall had hanged himself from the tree in
the backyard in November 1921. They described Rupert as
being a "tormented soldier."

Sandy Kendall had even shown the police a vial of
laudanum that he had found among his daughter's things.
There was a photograph of him holding the vial up for the
paper. Sandy was described as the son of a "northern banker"
who had followed in his father's footsteps. He was of stat-
uesque build and great height, towering over everybody at
the crime scene, including his distraught son Whalen.

I then put in a new microfilm for 1921 and found the
article about Rupert Kendall. The headline read, "The

Great War Claims Yet Another Life." Straight up, the article portrayed Rupert as disturbed and unable to live within society since returning from France. He'd participated in the second Battle of the Somme, where American casualties were enormous. The article also said that Rupert had not returned to Missouri directly after the war, and for months nobody knew where he was. Finally, he returned home and literally never left the sanctuary of the grounds on Haggeman Road.

Neighbors talked of seeing him sitting on the front porch; occasionally he would sit in the backyard and stare at the giant oak tree—the tree where they had found his body. Other neighbors claimed to have heard screaming from the house. They said that upon visiting, they would find Rupert "unruly," "angry," and "wild."

One woman told a story of how her dog had become ill and, rather than let the dog suffer, her husband had put it out of its misery by shooting it in the backyard. According to the woman, when Rupert heard the gunshot, he jumped off of the porch and ran around the yard screaming. It had taken his sister, Glory, two hours to coax him out of his hiding place behind the shed.

The thing that struck me the most was the fact that Rupert hadn't shot himself at all. He'd hanged himself. Which meant that either the blood in his room was due to an incident that had not resulted in Rupert's death, or it belonged to somebody else. Possibly his brother, Whalen.

Finding the report of Whalen's suicide would take more time. I knew it had to have happened sometime between June and December of 1922, but not knowing exactly when meant that I had to skim each paper or chance passing it up. I could almost bet that Whalen's suicide would make the front page, since he was the last child of the family and the third to have ended his life tragically within one year's time. I mean, what editor wouldn't have put that on the front page?

Sure enough, August of 1922, I found it on the front page. The headline read, "Third Tragedy to Strike Kendall Family." August! That meant Sandy Kendall's children had all taken their own lives within nine months. Nine months! In the time it took to bring a new life into the world, an entire family had checked out. It was overwhelming, nearly more than I could stand.

I read the article on Whalen with great interest, since I really didn't know anything about him. There was a photograph of him with a smaller photograph of each of his siblings. The author spent a great deal of time pondering the same damn questions I had been pondering. What the hell had happened? Whalen, it appeared, had served in the military as well, but had never seen front-line carnage like Rupert. According to his father, Whalen didn't have to go to war, since he was married and his wife was pregnant, but he insisted it was the right thing to do and went off anyway. Interestingly, although he didn't leave until after Rupert had left, he returned within six months. Whalen and his wife lived next door to Sandy and Glory during his brother's absence in France. After Whalen's wife gave birth to a daughter, his wife unexpectedly took the child and up and left in the middle of the night. No note, no word as to where she had gone or why. Whalen sold his house and moved back in with his father and sister. This would have been about 1919, just before Rupert returned. Neighbors painted Whalen as a dutiful son who had given up everything for his father and brother. Evidently, he'd had plans to leave for New Orleans to start over and begin a business venture, but when Rupert returned, Whalen realized there was no way he could leave his father and Glory to deal with Rupert on their own.

According to the article, Whalen had shot himself in his brother's room.

I sat back and rubbed my eyes. Then I sighed and hit the print button. I left the library a few minutes later with my photocopies documenting three young lives gone horribly wrong.

I called Stephanie once again. "Steph, is Geena there yet?"

"Yes, she got here about half an hour ago," she said.

"Would you guys like me to bring you back some lunch?"

"Oh, sure, where are you going?"

"I thought about hitting Steak-n-Shake," I said.

"I want a steakburger and a strawberry shake. And…" There was a pause as she waited for Geena to decide what she wanted to eat. "Geena wants a steakburger and a large caffeine."

"Okay," I said.

"Oh, and she wants an order of fries."

"Good."

"And a bowl of chili."

I laughed. "You think she's hungry?"

"Just a bit," she said with humor in her voice.

I stopped and got our lunch and then drove back to New Kassel with my car smelling like grease and onions. I know that sounds gross, but it actually smelled really good.

When I entered the Gaheimer House, Geena was

coming down the stairs, pulling her white gloves off. Stephanie called out, "Back here!" I motioned for Geena to meet me in the kitchen, where we all sat around and ate our lunch. I had a turkey club with fries.

"So what's the deal with the quilts?" Stephanie asked, taking a drink of her shake.

I explained to her about the Kendall house and Glory Kendall and my plan to purchase all of the quilts, even if I didn't get the house.

"How exciting," she said. "Something new in town. That'll shake everybody up."

"What did you learn today?" Geena asked.

I filled her in on most of my discoveries, then stopped and wondered about a few things out loud. "It still makes no sense to me, though. Rupert killed himself first, in November of '21, and yet around Christmas Glory begins quilting again, and she makes this big deal of stating how her legacy is her quilts. I mean, you get the feeling that she was on the comeback, not spiraling the other way. Then she ends her life in June with an unfinished quilt in the frame. Does that make sense?"

Geena shook her head and thought about it. "Not really," she said.

"Also, Rupert hanged himself."

"But the blood?"

"There's blood?" Stephanie asked.

"It's his brother's. For some reason Whalen chose to shoot himself in Rupert's room," I said. "The more I dig, the more questions I come up with."

"Isn't that the way it always works?" Stephanie said, smiling.

"True," I said. "I'm going to check the St. Louis County library this week. Something of this magnitude would have drawn the attention of the St. Louis papers."

"I would think so," Geena agreed.

"Maybe those papers could shed a little more light on the why of this whole situation."

"What did you learn about the quilts?" Geena asked.

"Oh, my gosh. I almost forgot! Glory quilted probably fifty quilts in her life. We recovered how many?"

"Nine finished, and the one in the frame for sure," Geena said.

"Well, a few of the others without initials might be hers, as well. She documented who received her quilts as gifts, that's the cool part. And," I said, pulling a sheet of paper out of my back pocket, "I have descriptions of quilts that her mother and grandmother made, and one by her great-grandmother. So we should be able to see if any of the quilts we recovered are those."

"Let's go see," she said. "I can't wait another second. I want to see if I'm right."

After we washed our hands, all three of us hurried up the steps to the second floor, where Geena had spread whichever quilt she was studying on the full-sized poster bed.

"This one I'm looking at now I would say was made in the late 1840s. It's a coxcomb design made in red and green on a white background," she said.

"Why is there only a border on three sides?" Stephanie asked.

"Well, you have to understand, back then, most quilts were never going to be hung on a wall. They were made for the bed. The missing border is the top of the quilt that would either be hidden under pillows or pulled over the pillows and tucked down by the headboard. You'd never see it. You'll also find some quilts that have what looks like two missing square pieces at the bottom. Those were to accommodate the posters at the end of the bed."

"Oh," I said. "Makes sense."

I checked my notes. Glory had written about a green and red coxcomb made by her great-grandmother on her way from Rhode Island to what is now Michigan, sometime in the 1840s. "You're exactly right," I said.

"How'd you do that?" Stephanie asked Geena.

"A lot of it's about knowing what patterns were popular."

"I could make a coxcomb quilt right now," I said. "I'd probably pull my hair out in the process, since it's appliquéd, but I could do it now. How can you tell it wasn't made forty or however many years after that design went out of fashion?"

"That's when you have to rely on knowing what fabrics were available, what oxygen and light do to certain materials over time, dyes, that sort of thing. You know how there were no true yellow roses before a specific year?"

"No, I didn't know that," I said.

"Well, I can't remember the year, but it took breeding and a freak of nature to get a true yellow rose to happen," she said. "Same thing with colors of dyes and fabrics. Today we can create any color fabric we want, but not so a century ago. At one time there was a definite limited color palette. There was no fuchsia or chartreuse for an eighteenth-century quilter. So one way to document the age of a quilt is to know what colors were available, how the colors were made, and what effect time and elements have on each color."

"Oh," I said, feeling really stupid.

"The brown in that quilt over there was most likely a brilliant green at one time."

"So this one belonged to her great-grandmother," I said.

"Yes, what was her great-grandmother's name?" Geena asked.

"I don't know, but that I can find out," I said. I might not be able to date fabric, or know when a yellow rose was first developed, but by golly, I could hunt down somebody's great-grandmother.

"What about crazy quilts?" Stephanie asked.

"You won't find one of those prior to 1876, and very few were made after 1900 or 1910. Until, of course, they came into fashion again. I just made one last year."

Stephanie smiled. "Can we keep her?" she asked me.

I laughed and was about ready to say something when the doorbell rang. "I'll get it."

I went down the stairs and opened the door. It was Maddie Fulton.

"Maddie, what a nice surprise."

She handed me a big bouquet of roses, which I, of course, buried my nose in. It's the first thing you do when you see a rose. Stick your nose in it. Of course, that's the first thing I do with almost everything. At least according to my husband.

"Come in," I said, and stepped aside for her. "What brings you here?"

"I wanted to say thank you for all the hard work you've put into the rose show. All of the advertisements, setting up booths, the whole bit," she said.

"Oh, Maddie, that's my job," I said.

"Well, I still want to thank you," she said. "I also wanted to let you know that I'm getting the quilts together that

Glory gave my grandmother. The more I think about it, the more I really want you to display them."

"Oh, of course," I said. "At the very least, I want to get photographs of them." Maddie looked like she had something else on her mind, but she didn't say anything. "Would you like to see the ones we recovered from the Kendall house?"

"I'd love to, just some other time," she said. "I'm on my way to a garden club meeting."

"Oh, hey, was your grandmother's name Elspeth Bauer?"

"Yes," she said, looking surprised. "How did you know that? And why do you want to know?"

"Glory mentioned your grandmother in her quilt journal. Nothing major, she just mentioned giving Elspeth some of her quilts," I said.

"I think I have a few photographs of my grandmother and Glory together," she said. "I'll look those up for you, too."

"Did your grandmother ever mention Glory? I mean, other than the fact she'd given her the quilts?"

"You want to know what happened in that house, don't you?" she asked.

"Yes," I admitted.

"I can tell you some of what my grandmother knew, but I don't think she shared everything with me. I don't have time to go into it all right now. Why don't you come by later tonight or tomorrow, and I'll tell you."

"Okay," I said.

"Just suffice it to say that my grandmother never trusted the brother," she said.

"Rupert?"

"No, Whalen," she said. "I don't have time right now. But there is one other thing I wanted you to know."

"What's that?"

"I think somebody was in my house last night," she said. "The back door was cracked when I got up."

"Could the wind have knocked it open?"

"No, it's a sliding glass door," she said.

"Have you told the sheriff?"

"No," she said, as if that had never occurred to her. "I'm telling you."

I chuckled a bit. "Was anything taken?"

"Not that I can tell, but I know somebody was there. I could tell by the garden."

"The garden?"

"Whoever it was broke off one of my elephant ears and trampled my Graham Thomas."

"Your what?"

"It's a rosebush," she said. "Lovely fragrance. A yellow blush color."

"Oh."

"Look, I need to go and get this meeting over with. It's gonna take a lot out of me, you know. Eleanore will be there."

I rolled my eyes. "Sorry."

She turned to go and I stopped her. "Hey, what year was the first yellow rose?"

"Oh, uh…well, if you mean a true bright yellow rose, that would be right around 1900. A man named Joseph Permet-Ducher had been breeding roses trying to come up with a true yellow and had failed up to that point. Then one day he was walking through a field and there was a mutant. A yellow rose. He used that rose to produce yellow and orange roses, and we've had them ever since."

I smiled and waved to her as she left. Then I put my bouquet of freshly cut roses in a vase and put it in the sitting room. I didn't want them all the way back in the kitchen where nobody could see them. I had no idea what sort of rose they were, what fancy names they had or anything of the sort. As I looked at the vase all I was thinking was *Pink, white, oooh sorta pink and white together. Fat, fluffy. Pretty*. That was good enough for me.

Just as I was about go back upstairs, the front door to the Gaheimer House opened and Colin walked in. "Hey," I said. "What's up?"

"Your mother wants me to head over to the garden club meeting," he said. "In case there's any excitement."

"You're not the sheriff anymore," I said.

"Yeah, but I'm bigger than all of them, so if they start any crap I can…I don't know, stand up and look menacing, I guess."

I laughed. Leave it to my mother.

"How's it going on that Kendall thing?" he asked.

"It's going. I've been finding out a lot of new stuff."

"Oh, yeah?" he asked. "Like what?"

"You don't have time to hear it all. You've got a meeting to go to," I said.

"Right," he said. He looked utterly dejected. At one time he would have been right in the thick of things, giving me warnings and telling me how much of a pain in the butt I was. Now he was attending garden club meetings.

"You want to come with me?" he asked.

"Not really," I said. "I try to avoid Eleanore if at all possible."

"Okay, well, I'll let you know if there's any excitement," he said.

"You do that, Colin," I said.

NINE

RUDY, THE KIDS, and I were all seated at Velasco's Pizza later that evening. Not only is the pizza really good, but the owner, Chuck Velasco, is one of Rudy's best friends and his bowling partner. So we try to eat here once a week to support one of our own. It has absolutely nothing to do with the fact that I hate to cook. Nothing at all.

Velasco's is done in a 1950s décor, and Chuck himself takes orders, cooks pizzas, and fraternizes with the customers. He wears flannel plaid shirts and work boots nearly every day, except in the summer. He looks like he should be driving a backhoe rather than flipping pizzas, but he confided in me one day that he'd always wanted to be a chef. Chuck has a temper, too. We were eating dinner here one night several years back when he threw the glass cookie jar at his ex-wife.

"Hey, guys!" Chuck called out from behind the counter.

We all waved. Matthew was busy tearing up his paper napkin with his fork, while Mary was preening, running her hands through her hair every five seconds. I realized that Tony, the adorable Italian boy who was in her class, was sitting by the window with his family. The great thing about Rachel having a steady boyfriend was that she didn't preen quite so much anymore. Once she realized that Riley liked her regardless, she even stopped wearing eyeliner. Wonders never cease.

"Mom, can I dye my hair black?" Mary asked.

"Why would you want to do that?" Rudy asked.

"I'm asking Mom," she said.

Rudy shot her a death look, and I said, "Hey, watch your mouth."

"Oh, like he's gonna know what color would look good on me," she said. "I'm asking you. Because even though you're old, you at least have some taste."

She was thirteen. I had seven years to go until she was twenty. I was not so sure I would make it without killing her.

"Really," I said. "Like what?"

"You have excellent taste in shoes," she said.

"Oh, thanks," I said.

"Don't get a big head," she said. "Please, I wanna dye my hair black."

Here's the dilemma we face as parents of today's teenagers. Did I want my thirteen-year-old to dye her hair black? No, of course not. She's got gorgeous blondish hair with little coppery highlights. Like I want that ruined? No. Her hair is also naturally curly, but she straightens it every morning. As much as I wanted her to inherit curl from her father instead of the straight boring stuff that I have, she wants just the opposite. Straight-as-a-poker hair is in right now. Anyway, did I want to make a big deal out of something that would last a couple of months and grow out? No. The trick is to pick and choose your battles. Would it hurt anything if she dyed her hair black? No, although she'd probably ruin at least two towels in the process. On the other hand, will it hurt if she goes to a rave party? Yes. So, see, I have to choose which battles are the most important, because if I just shoot her down on everything, she'll rebel.

I had to make her think that I didn't want her to dye her hair and was giving in only under great pressure so that she would think she'd won some huge major battle, so that later when she actually loses a big major battle it won't be such a big deal to her. In actuality, as much as I don't want her to have black hair, in the grand scheme of things, black hair is no big deal. Pierced noses are no big deal, either. Tattooed face? Big deal.

"Please?" she asked with her hands clasped together.

"We'll see," I said.

"We will?" Rudy asked. I tried to tell him to shut up with my eyes, but that never works with him.

Mary slumped. "'We'll see' always means no."

"No, it doesn't," I said.

"Although it probably does in this case," Rudy said, glaring at me.

"She just wants her hair black so she can be different," Rachel said. "Nobody at her school has black hair. Well, except for Lexy, but hers is natural. Nobody has fake black hair."

"Whatever," I said.

"You just need to shut up," Mary said to Rachel.

"Oh, and who is gonna make me?"

"Stop," Rudy said.

"I'll come right over there and make you," Mary countered.

"You and what army?" Rachel asked.

"Oh, jeez," I said. "Stop. Eat. Next person that says a word gets grounded from the computer."

Both girls just looked at each other and made faces.

"That means talking with your face, too."

"I wanna be a spy when I grow up," Matthew said.

Just then Eleanore came bursting into Velasco's—you know, I've noticed that Eleanore never really enters a room in any other way other than bursting. Something told me she was here to see me. Maybe it was the fact that she headed straight for my table. Maybe it was the way she barreled over two waitresses and three-year-old Tommy Burgermeister to get to my table.

"Uh-oh," Rudy said.

"That woman is not right," Mary said. "She looks like a giant strawberry."

Yes, she did have on her strawberry outfit today. She usually reserves that for the Strawberry Festival. Maybe everything else was dirty. "Torie!"

"Yes, Eleanore," I said.

"Your stepfather told me to shut my face."

I couldn't help it. I burst into laughter, as did Mary and Rachel. Rudy tried to remain stoic, and Matthew was too busy killing his napkin to notice anything. "I'm glad you think that's funny."

"Sorry," I said.

"It's the way you said it," Rachel said.

Eleanore's icy gaze nearly wilted Rachel on the spot. My daughter went back to eating her pizza.

"Sorry," I said. "Start from the beginning."

Eleanore pulled a chair from the table next to us and straddled it like a horse. "We were at the garden club meeting, which he is not even a member of, but anyway, and all I did was give my opinion on the rose show— which by the way, I have over thirty-seven callers voting for Mister Lincoln—and Colin jumped up and said,

'Eleanore, shut your face.' Well, let me tell you, I was never so insulted in all my life. So I asked him what gave him the right to even be at the meeting and he said, and I quote, 'I am acting within the official capacity of the office of mayor.' What in Hades does that mean, exactly?"

"It means Colin is bored stiff and wants his old job back," I said.

"Torie," Rudy said.

"Well, he does," I said.

"You tell your mother to keep a tighter leash on him," Eleanore said. "I was never so embarrassed. In front of all of my garden friends!"

"Colin is not on a leash," I said.

Although my mother had insisted that he go to the meeting in the first place. I smiled to myself to think that maybe my mother does keep Colin on a leash. Of course, I think there's no place that Colin would rather be than on the end of a string held by my mother.

"Then your mother better get one," Eleanore said. She took a piece of pizza from our table. "Because I will not stand for this. People can't just publicly humiliate somebody else and get by with it. They can't just behave like that and think it's okay." She took a big bite out of the slice of pepperoni and mushroom pizza, put the chair back, and left the restaurant with her confiscated food.

"I really hate that woman," Mary said.

"That's not nice," I said. Rudy's eyes were smiling at me, because he knew Mary had said what I really wanted to say.

After dinner was over, Rudy paid the bill and met us outside. "Can we stop by Maddie Fulton's on the way home?" I said.

"Sure, as long as it's fast, because I'm meeting the guys to go bowling in half an hour. Why?"

"She has some information for me. Plus, I want to hear her side of what happened at the garden club meeting. I think Eleanore and Colin's stories are both going to be slightly one-sided," I said. "Besides, it'll only take a minute."

"Okay," he said.

We drove through town with the windows down, and a warm, moist spring breeze tickled our faces through the open windows. It would have been an exceptionally calm and serene moment if it hadn't been for Mary in the backseat saying, "Stop touching me."

"Chill," Rachel said.

"He won't stop touching me," Mary said. "Tell him to stop touching me."

"Matthew, stop touching Mary," I said.

"Mom! Do something! He won't stop touching me," Mary cried in hysterics.

"For the love of God, Matthew, stop touching your sister," I said.

"Is this the house?" Rudy asked.

"Yes," I said. "I'll just be a minute." I jumped out of the car—I couldn't get out of there fast enough—and left Rudy to deal with the kids.

The lights were on in Maddie's house, but she didn't answer the door when I knocked. I knocked again. I could hear Mary screaming from the car and Rudy yelling something about sleeping in the stables with the horses. I tried the doorknob, and it was unlocked.

"Torie, do not go in that house," Rudy called out from the car window.

"I'll just be a minute." I was a bit worried about her, since she wasn't answering the door. If I entered and she was indecent, I would apologize until the cows came home, but if there was something wrong, she'd be eternally grateful. I took the chance and entered the house. "Maddie? It's me, Torie."

She wasn't in the living room or the kitchen, so I headed down the hallway toward the bedrooms. In the first bedroom on the left, I found Maddie lying on the floor with the phone knocked off the hook. Her face was locked in a horrible grimace, and spittle ran from her mouth. Her back arched, she was in the throes of some sort of seizure. "Oh, Jesus," I said. I flipped open my cell phone and called the sheriff's office directly.

"Mort, it's Torie. Get an ambulance out to Maddie Fulton's house right away, and I mean fast. Break the sound barrier if you have to."

Just then I heard Mary's voice getting louder and louder. "I cannot live one more day with that freak you call a daughter," she said, rounding the corner. "Oh, gross."

"Get out of here, Mary."

"Mom? What's the matter with her?"

"Get out!"

"Mommy?" Then she burst into tears.

THE AMBULANCE WAS there within five minutes.

Followed by Sheriff Mort.

Followed by Colin.

Colin entered the house as if he owned the place. "What are you doing here?" I asked him.

"I heard the call go out," he said.

"You heard—Colin, do you have a police radio on at home?"

"Doesn't everybody?" he asked.

I shook my head as he tried to see around me into the hallway. I placed a hand on his shoulder. "Look, this is Mort's crime scene," I said. "Don't do anything to step on his toes."

"What?" he asked. He gazed at me with a faraway look in his eyes. Then reality set in. "Oh. Right. As mayor, I just thought I should be here. What do you think happened?"

"I don't know. It looks like some sort of seizure."

"Is Maddie an epileptic?" he asked.

"I was just getting ready to ask the same thing," Mort said as he walked toward us from the bedroom where I'd found Maddie.

"Not that I know of. I don't really know her that well," I said. "She doesn't wear a bracelet or anything, does she?"

"Didn't find one. I've found nothing in her medicine cabinets that indicates she was taking any medicine for epilepsy. Or any medicine at all. I found some Aleve and some Robitussin. That was it," Sheriff Mort said.

"Medicine cabinet, that's good," Colin said. "Good to check there."

Mort gave him a sideways glance and directed his conversation to me. "Tell me what you were doing here."

I told him about stopping by to get some information from her. "I just found her like that," I said.

Mort motioned me back to the bedroom, and Colin followed, nearly bumping into me. "Be careful where you step. What do you see here?" Mort asked.

"Well, she obviously went for the phone," I said.

The bed was made, and on it, I assumed, was one of Glory

Kendall's quilts. It was an unfinished project, pin-basted to the batting but not yet quilted. Maddie had mentioned she was getting the quilts together to give to me for the display. There was a pile of dirty laundry in the corner of the room and a still-life painting on the wall; the nightstand held a glass of water, some straight pins, a hairbrush, and a telephone. "I don't know what you want me to see," I said.

"If it was a real seizure, she wouldn't have had time to react to get to the phone. Some epileptics, if they've been epileptics for a long time, can sometimes tell when a seizure is about to come on. But for a seizure to just hit a person who's never had one—she honestly wouldn't have been able to get to the phone."

"Maybe she knocked it off the hook accidentally," Colin said. "In the violence of the seizure."

"I'm thinking that's more plausible," Mort said.

"If it's not epilepsy, what are you suggesting?" I asked.

"Poison," Colin said.

"It's too early to tell—and she could have had a seizure—but my gut instinct is with Colin on this one. Poison," Mort said.

"What?" I said. The creepiest feeling overcame me. "But who? And why?"

Then my eyes grew wide. Mort and Colin both looked at me. "What?" Mort said.

"Maddie told me that somebody was in her house last night," I said. "Sheriff, you need to dust the sliding glass door in the kitchen for prints and…and…check the garden for shoe prints. Especially by the elephant ears and Graham Thomas."

"The what?" he asked.

I went to Maddie's bookshelf in the living room and

chose a book on roses. I checked the glossary for Graham Thomas and then flipped to the page. "A rosebush that looks like this," I said.

"All right," Mort said. "I've already called the hospital and the ambulance, telling them I suspect poison. Hopefully, you got here in time and they can give her an antidote."

"What kind of poison do you think it was?" I asked.

"Strychnine," Colin said.

"Exactly," Mort said. "It's the only kind of poison I know of that makes the back arch like that. Which is why I think it was poison instead of a medical condition. She wasn't having a seizure when I saw her. She was locked in this position."

"Strychnine?" I said. My voice sounded hollow, and my fingers tingled.

"It's a really nasty way to die," Mort said.

"Die? She's gonna die?" I asked.

"Not necessarily. I think you got here just as it happened," Mort said. "Plus, I don't know how big of a dose she got. It takes less than seven or eight drops to kill you, but there's a chance…she might live."

"Might?" I asked.

"Who would do such a thing?" Sheriff Mort said.

Colin inclined his head as though willing me to read his thoughts. Evidently it worked. "No, not Eleanore," I said.

"Eleanore?" Mort asked.

"Eleanore Murdoch," I said. "She and Maddie have been arguing over this stupid rose show, but honestly, Eleanore wouldn't hurt a fly."

"Well, it wasn't a fly that was poisoned," Sheriff Mort said. "It was a woman."

TEN

THE NEXT DAY, after lunch, I was at the Gaheimer House helping Geena with the Kendall quilts when the sheriff came by to see me. Mort entered the house with his hat in his hand. There wasn't a line or a crease anywhere on his uniform. It was almost as if he hadn't sat down since he'd gotten dressed. His violet eyes looked worried. "Torie, I, uh…"

"What?" I asked. "How's Maddie?"

"She made it through the night. She's unconscious right now. They're keeping her that way. I'm pretty sure she's going to make it. Evidently, she didn't get enough of the poison to kill her. I've no idea when she'll be able to speak and talk with me, though."

"Oh, thank God," I said. "Was it strychnine?"

"Yes," he said. "Absorbed through the skin. Not ingested."

"Oh," I said, because, well, I wasn't sure what else to say to that.

"The prints on the sliding glass door were Eleanore Murdoch's," he said. "We're checking the shoe prints in the garden with all of the shoes in her closet."

I was speechless. I felt for the chair behind me as my mouth went dry. I never actually sat down, though. That would have taken far too much concentration.

"She's being arrested as we speak," he said.

"Deputy Miller is doing the deed."

"I don't believe this," I said. "Eleanore is arrogant, flighty, petty—and, yeah, sometimes she has a bit of a mean streak, but attempted murder? My God, Mort, I don't think Eleanore could figure out how to get her hands on strychnine! She's not the sharpest tack in the box."

"Well, she's got motive and her prints are on the back door and you said yourself that Maddie had told you somebody had been in her house the night before," he said.

"Motive?" I shrieked. "What *motive?*"

"The rose show," he said. "Something about rose selections. The whole town is talking about it."

I laughed. "Oh, that is preposterous," I said. "If Eleanore would try to kill Maddie over a rose, she would have killed me a long time ago. We've butted heads on so many issues, it's not funny. It's also no secret. I mean, honestly, Mort. She'd have more motivation to kill me than she would Maddie, and I'm still here."

Colin came in the door at that moment, gazed around the room, found Mort and me, and said, "You're arresting Eleanore."

"Yes," Mort said.

"Damn," Colin said. "I've always wanted to arrest that woman."

"It doesn't make sense," I said. "If Eleanore broke into Maddie's house to kill her, don't you think she would have worn gloves?" I said.

"Not necessarily. Maybe it didn't occur to her to wear gloves because she never thought the death would be investigated as a homicide," he said.

"Well, if she's stupid enough to leave prints everywhere,

I don't think she'd be smart enough to kill Maddie," I said. I folded my arms as if there were nothing else to say.

"Nevertheless, Torie, I've got to make the arrest," he said.

My cell phone rang then. It was my mother. "Eleanore Murdoch's been arrested."

"I know," I said. "Mort is here now telling me. Let me call you back." I hung up. "There has to be something we're not seeing," I said to the guys. "You know, Maddie was supposed to give me information last night on the Kendall suicides."

"Uh-oh," Colin said.

Mort and I glared at him.

"This is the way it always starts," Colin said. "She finds some little connection, some little bitty thread to link today to back then, and then she won't let you rest until she builds a whole damn bridge."

"Do you mind?" I said to Colin. "Who let you in, anyway?"

"I don't understand what the century-old Kendall suicides have to do with anything," Mort said.

"Maybe nothing. I just find it strange that she'd tell me to come see her, that she had information, and then she ends up poisoned. A big coincidence," I said.

"Coincidences do happen," Mort said.

"Try telling her that," Colin said. "Just you try to tell her that."

"Colin, please go home. Or go chase a tiny ball around with a big stick," I said.

"Golf course is closed for some reason. A drainage issue," he said.

"That's not my problem," I said.

Just then Helen Wickland came in the front door, out of breath and panting. "They've just arrested Eleanore Murdoch," she said. I think she'd run all the way from the Murdoch Inn to the Gaheimer House to tell me the news.

"We know," all three of us said simultaneously.

"She's asking for you, Torie," Helen said.

I glanced at the sheriff. "Are you taking her to Wisteria?" He nodded.

"All right. Helen, will you go with me?" I asked.

"Of course," she said. "I'll even drive. Maybe I'll get to see Eleanore in a prison uniform. That would make my day."

Helen and I left Mort and Colin to twiddle their thumbs. Helen nodded to her car across the street and held up her keys. Helen loves to drive her little red Mini Cooper. In a town where you don't really need to drive anywhere, Helen would drive from her garage to the mailbox just for the sake of driving. On the drive to Wisteria we broke most of the speed limits all the way there. Except for when we approached the stray cow in the middle of the Outer Road, I don't think Helen braked at all.

"You know there's no love lost between me and Eleanore," Helen said.

"I know," I said, gripping the oh-shit bar as she took a turn at fifty.

"But there is no way that woman tried to kill Maddie," she said. "Besides, if she had tried to kill her, it would have been big and messy and out there. Poison is too subtle for Eleanore."

"I agree."

Helen took another turn on two wheels. "Eleanore would have made a production out of it."

"Yes, I agree again."

"Who would have a reason to want Maddie dead?" Helen said, shifting gears. "I can't think of anybody."

"I can't either, but then I don't know her all that well. Maybe it's a disgruntled lover that we know nothing about," I said. "It could be anybody for any number of reasons."

Helen whipped her car around into a parking space in front of the jail and stopped it on a dime, just an inch from the curb. She smiled at me. "Ever since I saw *Bourne Identity* I've wanted to do that," she said.

"I'm happy for you, Helen," I said. I straightened my hair and my shirt.

"What are you doing?"

"Just making sure I didn't lose anything on the ride over here."

She laughed at me, and then we went inside. "Hi, Ollie," I said as I approached the front desk. "I'm here to see Eleanore. They just brought her in."

"She's not allowed any visitors, you know that," he said.

"But she's asking for me."

"Are you her lawyer?"

"No," I said. I wondered whether if I'd said yes, I'd have had to prove it.

"Then you can't see her."

"When can I see her? You can't keep visitors from her forever."

"It could be hours," he said.

"I'll wait."

Helen agreed to come back and pick me up, since she'd left her store completely unmanned. My cell phone rang no fewer than thirteen times while I waited to see

Eleanore. I knew that Mort could let me see her, if he wanted to, but I wasn't going to make a scene. I'd be a good girl and wait patiently.

After five hours, I was ready to shake off all that good-girl crap I'd been feeding myself earlier and raise holy hell. Just as I stood to go ask to see Mort, my cell phone rang again. It was my house, which meant it was either Rachel calling to tell me some new exciting thing about the play, or it was Mary wanting something.

"Mom," Mary said.

"What?"

"What's for dinner?"

"What's for dinner?" I repeated. "Look, Mary, I don't have a clue what's for dinner. It's the least of my worries right now."

"But I'm hungry."

"So eat something."

"But I want dinner," she said.

"Mary, eat something. You'll get dinner."

"What are we having?" she asked.

"If you ask me one more time, I'm going to feed you pig's feet," I said.

"No, I'm being serious, Mom," she said.

"Like I'm not?" I yelled.

"Just tell me what's for dinner."

I hung up on her.

Mort came out of a door and motioned me toward him. "She's asking for you, so I'm going to let you speak to her," he said.

"All right," I said.

"Leave your purse here."

He took me back to the jail cells, which I'd seen for myself on two different occasions. The jail is gray cinder block, with that boring tile floor that they use in high schools. I've often wondered why they didn't use blues and pinks, since those colors are supposed to calm you down. Eleanore was sitting at the table in the visiting room, hand-cuffed. She was dressed in an orange jumpsuit, which didn't look out of place on her. I'd seen her wear worse many times.

"Hi, Eleanore," I said.

Eleanore looked up at me, tears staining her face. "I can't even wear a hat in this godforsaken place."

"Nope," I said. "Hats are not allowed."

"Well, at least orange is one of my colors," she said. What color wasn't her color? She wore them all. "You think where I'm going they'll have those striped outfits like they did in *O Brother?* Because stripes make me look bigger."

"Eleanore," I said, "quit talking like that. You're not going anywhere. You'll be home in no time." I couldn't believe that I was actually comforting Eleanore. "Tell me what happened," I added.

"Well, they stormed into the inn in front of all my guests! Then they read me my rights and handcuffed me. They were quite brutal about it, too."

"No, I mean, before that. Eleanore, your fingerprints were found on Maddie Fulton's back door," I said.

She took a deep breath and her chin began to tremble. "I went there to find her list," she said.

"What list?"

"The list of rose selections for the rose show," she said.

"I'd heard through the grapevine that she and the other rosarians had chosen twenty-five roses for the rose show, but she wouldn't tell us what they were. She said they would 'unveil' them at the show. That it was a surprise."

"And?" I asked.

"Well, of all the nerve!" she said. "Who does she think she is? So I snuck over to her house, went around the back, and opened the patio doors. They weren't locked. Stupid ninny had gone to bed without locking the patio doors. Of course, the gate to the yard had been locked. You know that big tall privacy fence she has... Well, there was a spare key in the impatiens bed. I knew that because I'd overheard her tell Amelia Stevens where she kept it. So I waited until she went to sleep, and then I went into her office and tried to find the list. I couldn't find it, so I left. Simple as that."

"That's it?" I asked.

"I didn't kill her, Torie."

"Well, nobody did," I said. "She survived. At least so far."

"Do you think she'll be out of the hospital in time for the rose show?"

"Eleanore!"

"Well, because somebody will need to take over for her, if not."

"Eleanore, please," I said. "Why did you want to see me?"

"Can you get Colin to pull some strings and get me out of here?" she asked. "I really didn't hurt her."

"You've admitted to breaking and entering," I said.

"Just entering. I used a key, and the back door was open. I didn't take anything, either. At the very worst it's trespassing."

I wasn't sure, but I thought she was technically correct.

I wasn't going to tell her that though. Her complete lack of shame was so…so…so typically Eleanore.

"I think I'm allergic to the detergent here," she said, scratching her neck vigorously.

"Eleanore, I just spent five hours waiting here to see you because I thought you had something important to tell me," I said.

"I did," she said. "I want you to talk to Colin about getting me out of here."

"Why didn't you just ask him yourself?"

"Because he likes you better than me," she said.

With that I stood and left her sitting at the table. Maybe a few days in an orange jumpsuit would do her some good. I wasn't going to "pull strings" for her, not if she paid me. She hadn't been petty enough to try to kill Maddie—that much I was sure of—but she'd been petty enough to put herself in a very precarious predicament, all for a stupid list of roses! As far as I was concerned, she could sit here until her lawyer got her out.

Besides, I didn't think Colin could pull any strings to get her out any sooner, because I didn't think there were any strings to pull. Mort was going by the book on this one, and I wasn't about to stop him. The woman was infuriating.

As I left the room, Mort stopped me. "Well?"

"She claims she went to Maddie's to find a list of roses. Says the back door was unlocked. She couldn't find the list, so she didn't even steal anything," I said. "Anyway, that's her side of the story."

"That's what she told me, too," he said. "Why did she want to see you so badly?"

"It was nothing," I said. "A waste of my time."

My cell phone rang. It was Mary.

"Mom, *please,* tell me what's for dinner."

THE NEW KASSEL GAZETTE
The News You Might Miss
By Eleanore Murdoch

I am, at this moment, writing to you from inside the jail cells of Granite County. Yes, folks, I am incarcerated for a crime that I did not commit. I am as innocent as new-fallen snow. As misunderstood as…well, a whole bunch. My fellow New Kasselonians, my hope is that none of you will ever see a Granite County jail cell from the view that I have at this moment. It is vile and dirty and gloomy. A little wallpaper would go a long way in this place.

At any rate, my husband, Oscar, is selling his homemade peach butter and blackberry jams at booth number seven this coming weekend. I hope you will all come by and support us, especially since, due to my current situation, we are sure to incur some outrageous legal fees.

I heard from the desk officer, who heard it from a local cabdriver (there's only three in all of Wisteria), who heard it from Colin, who heard it from his wife, that there may be a new owner of the old Kendall house in the next few months. And Torie O'Shea wanted me to ask, if anybody in town has any old quilts, letters, journals, or photographs pertaining to the Kendalls, from the Kendalls, or made by the Kendalls, that you please contact her at the Gaheimer House for a possible historical display of your artifacts. Now, I am off to contemplate the sunset!

                              Until next time,
                              Eleanore

ELEVEN

TWO DAYS AFTER Eleanore had been arrested, Maddie Fulton was still in a drug-induced coma. I'd spent those two days helping Geena Campbell with the Kendall quilts. Geena's work was finally finished, and she gave me an estimate on the net worth of the collection. I drove over to Evan Merchant's house to give him a check.

I knocked on his door, and Bon barked furiously from the back of the couch until Evan finally answered it. Evan looked a bit hungover, but maybe that's how he always looked in the morning.

"Hi, Evan," I said. "Here's your check for the quilt collection."

"Thank you," he said.

"I made an offer on the house yesterday."

He just nodded. "Look, Torie, I need for this house to be gone. It's an albatross around my neck, you know," he said. "But you're a nice person. Are you sure you can handle this house?"

"What do you mean?" I asked. "I know it's a bit rough around the edges, but I've worked very hard on the Gaheimer House. I think I can do this."

"That's not what I meant," he said and nodded toward the house.

I turned around and looked where he gestured.

"There used to be a big old tree standing in that yard."

"How do you know?" I said.

He shrugged. "I don't know much, except for what I've seen with my own eyes and a few things I've heard from people in town. That stump over there, that was the tree."

I wasn't sure where he was going with this, so I just let him talk.

"Her window"—he pointed—"is right in line with the tree."

"The shade is opened," I said, looking at him. "I closed it."

"Just as I have a hundred times," he said. "It never stays shut. So I stopped going in there to shut it."

I laughed nervously. "Evan…"

"I think she's looking out on the tree," he said. "Or what was the tree. I think she's looking *for* the tree. I don't know why."

"Evan, that's ridiculous," I said.

Putting his hands up in the air, he said, "I'm just telling you what I've seen with my own eyes. I don't want you buying this house and having it do to you what it's done to me."

"I'm sure I'll be fine," I said. "I was wondering, though. If you accept the offer, could I get back in the house before we actually close?"

"You can get in the house now, if you want. Just come and ask me," he said.

"Thanks," I said.

He glanced down at the check and smiled. "Damn, I never knew old blankets could be worth so much money."

I'm glad he was happy with the price Geena had put on them, because to me they were priceless.

I told him goodbye and headed up to the St. Louis County public library. I went to the headquarters on Lindbergh, across from Plaza Frontenac in a quiet, posh neighborhood. Even the local grocery store is fancy. Located in the western part of St. Louis County, it's a good forty-five minutes from where I live.

It was a warm day, high seventies. I wore jeans and a peach cotton blouse with flip-flops on my feet. I love having my toes free. I listened to some bluegrass on the radio as I drove.

At the library, I headed up to the special collections area. I waved to the librarians, who all waved back. I found a microfilm reader and looked up the World War I draft records, locating records for both Whalen and Rupert Kendall. Rupert was listed as the only son living at home, meaning Whalen had moved next door with his wife already. Rupert was listed as a shoemaker, five foot ten with blue eyes. Whalen was listed as a banker, five foot eight with green eyes. I printed both records and went to find the newspapers.

I knew the exact dates I was looking for, so the search was easy. Rupert's suicide was not even mentioned. This didn't surprise me. Why would St. Louis newspapers report a suicide of a man who lived in a different county if there was nothing unusual about it? St. Louis had enough of its own things to report. Glory's death was covered, though. The story had not been given front-page status, as it had in Granite County, but it had warranted one whole quarter-section of a page. As I suspected, it was because her brother had committed suicide less than seven months previously that the news made the St. Louis papers at all. Glory was described as "tall for a woman, thin, pretty, with a clear complexion and pure heart." I'm assuming the reporter was going by what acquaintances had said about her, because there was no way he could have known this himself.

The only unusual thing I found in the article was that the father and surviving brother had been so devastated that they hadn't reported the death for nearly a day. According to Whalen, "She'd been dead at least a day before we even realized anything was amiss. She often locked herself in her room, sewing." Then Sandy Kendall added, "We were so distraught…we sat with the body for half a day before calling the authorities. I couldn't bear for anybody to touch my baby girl."

Whalen's suicide also got print space. However, the article said very little, claiming that Sandy Kendall had been too shaken to give any sort of statement to the press. One neighbor was quoted as wondering whether or not Mrs. Whalen Kendall would return now that her daughter was the only living heir of Sandy Kendall.

How could I have been so dense? I'd gone right by the fact that Whalen's wife had left him and taken their daughter. What happened to the daughter? Sandy did not leave his estate to his granddaughter, and nobody had ever come to contest the will. In fact, I'd always heard that there were no living descendants of Sandy Kendall. Had Whalen's daughter grown up not knowing who she was? Had her mother never told her? Had Whalen's wife been so traumatized that she never looked back? Or had some tragedy befallen the granddaughter before 1956, when Sandy had died?

I sat back and scratched my head. Finding this girl

would be tough. If her mother changed their names, any census records they showed up in would be pointless. She'd probably remarried at some point. She could have gone anywhere in the country!

Wait. Think, think. I pulled out my cell phone and called the Gaheimer House.

My sister answered the phone. "Yeah?"

"Steph, it's me. I need you to check the Granite County marriages for me. Check for the years, oh…" Whalen had been born in 1891. It was a pretty good rule of thumb to check three years prior to the age of twenty-one and three years after for the subject's first marriage record. Not that people couldn't get married when they were younger or older, but historically speaking, most first marriages happened between the ages of eighteen and twenty-four. "1909 to 1915."

Considering his first child wasn't born until after he returned from the war, I'd almost bet he wasn't married until 1915.

"I need this now, Steph," I said.

"Sure. I'll get on it and call you back."

I put my cell phone on vibrate and then went to the restroom. Just as I was washing my hands, the phone buzzed.

It was Stephanie. "1915," she said. "Whalen Kendall married Hazel Schmid on September twenty-first. That's Schmid, not Schmidt. No *t*."

"Did her parents sign for her?" I said. "Oh, please say they signed for her."

"Her father did. Christophe Schmid."

"Hot damn," I said. "All right, thanks."

I ran back upstairs and found the 1910 census records.

After twenty minutes I found Christophe Schmid in the 1910 Soundex. I love the Soundex. It's coded by the person's last name, so you don't have to even know the county that the person lived in, only the state. Christophe's wife's name was Antonia. They had four children; one was Hazel, aged thirteen. The others were Ellie, Sam, and John. They lived in St. Charles County, the county directly west of St. Louis across the Missouri River. I couldn't help but wonder how Whalen had even met her, because St. Charles might be sixty to ninety minutes from New Kassel now, but back then, it would have probably been half a day's journey.

I then checked 1920, and Christophe and his wife were still in St. Charles County, although all of their children had left home. So I checked the 1920 Soundex for his two boys. One was in St. Charles. The other was in Audrain County, which is located pretty much in the middle of the state, a little north of the Missouri River.

I was ready to bet Hazel did one of two things, the same two things I would have done if I were a woman at the turn of the twentieth century with a new baby: I would have run home or gone off with another man. The other choices would have been prostitution, destitution, or giving up your child and striking out on your own—and unless you were one of the very, very few women of that time who were trained in an occupation, that meant menial, back-breaking labor in the factories. Why choose any of those if you had a lover to support you or a family that would help you get on your feet?

If she ran off with another man, I would never find her, unless somebody—currently alive—happened to know whom she left with, and I found those odds slim to none.

If she ran to her family, my chances of tracking her down improved. She would have known that Whalen would have checked with her father, which meant she would have gone to either her sister or to one of her two brothers. My bet would have been Sam, the one in Audrain County, the one farther away from Whalen. Provided, of course, she was the least bit worried that Whalen might be looking for her. I could have been wrong. Whalen may not have cared at all. She might have gone back to her father, because she knew Whalen wouldn't have been looking. It could have gone either way, really.

If she had gone to her brothers or her father, she and her baby did not appear on the 1920 Soundex in their households. Instead, I found Hazel Kendall listed in the household of one Ellie MacBride. That Ellie, I was almost certain, was Hazel's sister. That's the other great thing about the Soundex. Whoever you were searching for would show up by name, independently, and then the Soundex would tell you what family the person was living with. This did not always work, since, say, if your niece was staying with you, sometimes the census takers would list her with your last name. But if your ancestor was in a hospital, poorhouse, convent, or boardinghouse, or even just living with a family as a hired hand, during a Soundex census year—1890 through 1930—you could find that person quite easily, provided he or she were listed by last name. Whalen's daughter, Sophia, was listed as S. A. Kendall, and under the column that was for relationship to head of household, she was listed as niece. They were in Callaway County.

I knew there was a chance that, even if I did find any

descendants of Whalen's daughter, they wouldn't know anything about what I was looking for. Most people never talk about uncomfortable subjects, or mistakes they wish they hadn't made. No, they usually keep infuriatingly quiet about it.

How much easier my job would be if everybody wore their life's mistakes and secrets on their sleeves for me to check. Fantasy world. Oh well, I'm allowed to dream.

Most likely, the only way to find Hazel and her daughter would be to follow the line of the brothers to the present day, then call up their descendants and ask them if anybody knew what happened to Great-aunt Hazel. I could only follow the census trail to 1930, because the 1940 census was not yet available due to a seventy-five-year privacy act, and by 1930, any female descendants would have changed their last names, assuming they'd gotten married. That left me with male offspring of Hazel's brothers, Sam and John.

I could not find Hazel Kendall in the 1930 census. Most likely, she'd remarried. Nor was Sophie Kendall listed. I hoped that didn't mean she had died, that instead she'd been adopted by her mother's new husband. The 1930 census gave the names of Sam Schmid's children as Francis, three daughters, and then Henry. Henry was only two at the time, so it's possible that Sam had more children after 1930. John Schmid had Morgan, Ralph, two daughters, and then two more boys, Seth and Isaac. Now I just had to hope that at least one of these boys remained in the St. Charles and St. Louis area.

In the white pages, I found three Henry Schmids, one Ralph, and two Isaacs. I wrote down the phone numbers and addresses, stuffed the list in my pocket, and sighed heavily.

I gathered everything I had found, paid for copies, and then headed for home. Another day, I'd check the Callaway County marriages for Hazel Kendall, even though I could 't be sure that Hazel would have married in Callaway County, especially if her spouse had been from someplace else.

My head was swimming with all of this information by the time I got home. There was a note waiting for me on the kitchen table. It said that Rachel and Mary had gone to see Mrs. Hassler, the elderly neighbor across the road and down a half mile. They often go to Mrs. Hassler's to help her with her yard work. It ticks me off no end that my kids will work for a neighbor but won't even pick up their own dirty underwear without me having to threaten them. At least our neighbor, who needs the help, was getting it.

Matthew was still at my mother's house, and Rudy, I assumed, was still at work. I called Mrs. Hassler real quick to make sure that my kids were actually there. Call me paranoid, but how hard was it to leave a note saying you'd be with an old lady and actually be somewhere else? Huh? It scared me that I was thinking like a teenager. Mrs. Hassler answered on the third ring and confirmed the note on the table. I could almost hear Mary rolling her eyes on the other end of the line, because I'd been "lame" and checked up on them.

I grabbed an ice-cold Dr Pepper and some cheese to nibble on and went up to my office and sat down. The trees were all fully leafed out, and had been for a few weeks. They wouldn't seem this green in August, after they'd been baked by the sun all summer. I opened a window and let the spring air in, propped my feet up, and took a deep breath and a long drink of my soda. Then I saw on my desk a piece of paper that I'd jotted names on. Marty Tarullo and Judy Pipkin. They were the names Father Bingham had given me. Marty Tarullo still put flowers on Glory Kendall's grave every June. I decided that I would go see Marty, and possibly Judy, tomorrow.

Tonight I was going to veg. Right after I made some phone calls. I called the first Henry Schmid and got a recording. He sounded very young on the recording, so if he was related to the family I was looking for, he'd probably be a great-grandson. The second Francis answered.

I hate this part. Cold calling has never been my specialty, and people often think you're a quack when you say something like, "Excuse me, are you descended from Christophe and Antonia Schmid?" I've learned to sort of prep them a bit first.

"Hi, my name is Torie O'Shea, and I work for the historical society down in Granite County," I said.

"I'm not interested," he said.

"No, no, I'm not selling anything. Are you familiar with genealogy? It's where you trace your family tree?"

"Yes," he said cautiously. "I know what it is, but I've never done it."

"Well, I'm trying to track down a living descendant of a family that I'm working on. A Christophe and Antonia Schmid, who lived in St. Charles County at the turn of the twentieth century," I said.

He was quiet. "Is your family from St. Charles County?" I asked.

"My father is, but my mother was from Illinois."

"I'm actually looking for a descendant of their daughter,

but the male line is easier to follow because the last name never changes," I said.

More silence.

"Do any of these names sound familiar?" I gave him a list of Schmid family names that I'd found in the census.

"I don't think I can help you," he said.

"Okay, well, save me a phone call and let me know if the other two Henry Schmids in the phone book are related to you?"

"Oh, sure," he said. "The first one listed is not related. The second one is my father."

"Thanks for your help."

That's how it went. Name after name. Finally, I struck gold with Isaac. The grandson of Christophe and Antonia would have been seventy-eight or seventy-nine years old, depending on when in the year his birthday fell. I went through the whole spiel, and he admitted that Christophe had been his grandfather.

"Oh, great," I said. "That's fantastic. Okay, what I'm really after is what happened to your father's sister, Hazel Kendall. That would have been your paternal aunt."

"Ummmm," he said.

"See, on this end in Granite County, she just up and left one day and never came back. She had been married to a Whalen Kendall. I have no idea if you know it, but Whalen Kendall was a member of a family that had a tragic demise, and I was hoping that maybe Hazel's daughter could shed some light on what had happened," I said.

"Oh, yes…I always knew her as Aunt Mac," he said. His voice was raspy but clear, and I worried that his hearing was going bad, because he seemed to shout into the phone.

"Her husband's name was Tom MacBride, but we always called them Aunt and Uncle Mac. The only reason I connected it was because Aunt Mac's daughter's name was Sophia Kendall, and I always wondered why her last name was different. My mother told me not to question it. I know at some point Sophia started going by MacBride, because when she got married in the early forties, her wedding invitation said Sophia MacBride. I remember that clearly, because I asked my mother when she'd changed her name and my mother told me not to question such things. That it was rude." He gave a little chuckle then.

"Wait, Hazel married a MacBride? I thought her sister, Ellie, had been married to a MacBride," I said.

"Yes, Aunt Mac married Aunt El's brother-in-law. I don't know why we never called Aunt El 'Aunt Mac,' since technically she woulda been an Aunt Mac, but she'd just always been Aunt El."

So, when Hazel had gone to stay with Ellie, she'd come to fancy her sister's brother-in-law. I had run across siblings marrying siblings quite a few times while tracing family trees.

"So Sophia is your cousin, then," I said. "Is she still alive?" The chances were pretty slim, since she would have been born around 1919. She'd be pushing ninety. Not impossible, but I wouldn't count on it, either.

"No, in fact, she passed away about eleven years ago," he said.

"Did she have any children?" *Please say she had children.*

"Yeah," he said. "Seven of them. One lives in Boston. Two are in Chicago."

"Any of them live around here?" I asked.

"Yeah," he said. "Renee is here in town."

"In St. Charles?"

"Yeah," he said. "The other one, Anna, lives down by you. Around Wisteria, or maybe it's that other little town."

I almost dropped the phone. "In Wisteria?"

"Yeah, Anna Gatewood."

"Oh, my God," I said. "I know Anna Gatewood." And she didn't live in Wisteria, she lived in New Kassel.

"Ain't it a small world?" he said.

"Well, Mr. Schmid, thank you so much for talking to me," I said.

"Any time," he said. "Glad I could be of help."

You know, this whole naming scheme of the western world is just all wrong. Do you know how much easier all of that would have been if women didn't change their last names when they got married? I was mentally drained. It had taken me eight hours to learn that a woman I knew in town was the very person I'd been looking for.

I heard the front door slam, and Mary came running up the stairs to my office. She was gasping for breath by the time she reached the top stair. I was amazed she hadn't had a heart attack, since she'd just run half a mile; most of the time, she can't even sit up straight on the couch, much less actually run.

"Hi, Mom. What's for dinner?"

Maybe I'd just leave home.

TWELVE

I WAS ABSENT THROUGH most of dinner. I'd managed to pull together stuff for chicken fajitas, and I'd made brownies the night before. Even though I was seated at the table with my family, I wasn't really there. I kept thinking about Anna Gatewood. During our festivals Anna had set up many, many booths with literature on the gray wolf, the brown bear, and the lynx. All endangered species, all near and dear to her heart. She was the local animal rights and conservation activist. She worked at the animal hospital in Wisteria and at one point had almost fifteen strays staying in her house. Then her husband, Blake, stepped in and told her that she had to keep it to a maximum of five animals in the house. She was in a depression for nearly six months afterward.

She was about four years older than I was, maybe five. She must have been the youngest of Sophia Kendall MacBride's children, because Sophia would have been almost forty when she had Anna. Technically, Anna and her siblings were entitled to the Kendall house. Why hadn't she said anything before now? I wasn't even sure if there was anything she could legally do about her inheritance, fifty years after Sandy Kendall's death.

"It just seems odd," I said out loud.

Rachel and Mary exchanged glances and then laughed.

"What?" I said.

"You're thinking out loud again, honey," Rudy said.

"Oh, sorry," I said.

"So, what seems odd?" Mary said.

"Anna Gatewood is the granddaughter of Whalen Kendall," I said to Rudy.

"Whalen Kendall being?"

"One of the three siblings that I've been telling you about."

"Really?" he asked, plopping sour cream on his tortilla shell.

"I just think it's odd she hasn't mentioned it," I said.

"Oh, I don't know," he said. "It's not exactly an ice-breaker you'd use at a party. 'Oh, hello, I'm the grand-daughter of the man whose entire family committed suicide.' I mean, think about it," he said.

"Yeah, guess you're right," I said. I ate some more and totally spaced out, unable to follow the conversation that was going on right in front of me.

"Go," Rudy said.

"Huh? Go where?" I asked.

"Go see Anna," he said. "You won't sleep or anything until you do. You know you'll lie awake all night thinking about it, and by morning you'll have some cockamamie conspiracy theory all worked out and get yourself all in a tizzy. So go see her now and get it over with."

"I can't tell if I find it a comfort that you know me that well, or if it's really scary."

"It's really scary," he said. "I've damn near left you a hundred times." He winked at me, and I knew he was joking.

I finished eating and then headed over to Anna Gatewood's house. She lives on the street behind where my old house used to be on River Pointe Road. In fact, from my old bedroom window, I could just make out the chimney on her house. The lights were on and there was a car in the driveway.

I knocked, and Anna's husband answered the door. "Hi, Blake," I said. "I was wondering if I could talk with Anna."

"Well, sure, come on in," he said. "I don't think she can work the rose show, though. She's on double duty at the vets' office until they get another person hired."

"Oh, it's not about the rose show," I said.

"Anna! Torie's here to see you."

She came into the living room wiping her hands on a towel. She's about five foot six and never wears makeup. You have to respect that. She comes across as young, with short hair cut right at the ear in one of those swoop-bobs. "Torie," she said. "Nice surprise."

I often wondered if people really meant that when they saw me or if they were saying internally, *Oh, God, not her again. What does she want this time?*

"I was wondering if there was somewhere we could talk?" I said.

A worried expression crossed her face, and she glanced over her shoulder to where her husband had been moments before. "What about?" she said. "We can talk here. Would you like to have a seat? Do you want some tea? Or lemonade?"

"No, thank you," I said. I sat on her sofa, and she took the chair across from me. Her house was done in warm reds and browns, and there was an incredible smell of baked cinnamon and dough. It was the type of house that you could get comfy in. I like that kind of house. Then my purse was attacked by a Siamese cat, and a basset hound that was hidden under the table growled at me, and I thought that maybe her house wasn't so comfy after all.

"Don't pay any attention to them," Anna said. "If the cat goes for your hair, thump her on the head."

"Oh, great," I said. "Um…Anna, do you have a cousin named Isaac Schmid?"

"He's my mother's cousin," she said. "Haven't seen him since my sister got married…back in '85. Why?"

"I'm just making sure I've got the right Anna Gatewood," I said.

"What's this about?" she said.

"How much do you know about your mother's family?" I asked.

I was giving her the opportunity to tell me about the Kendalls on her own. If she didn't mention them, then I'd have to ask. "My grandma's family lived in St. Charles County. German, I think. That's about it really. Oh, my grandpa was an auto mechanic."

"Your mother's name was Sophia, right?"

"How did you know that?" she asked.

"All right," I said. "Just hear me out before you say anything. I've been doing some research on the Kendall family here in town."

If she was hiding the fact that she was related to the Kendalls, she was doing a great job. Her expression never changed, except she raised her eyebrows. "The, uh…the suicide family?"

"Yes," I said, thinking how horrible it would be to forever be known as the "suicide family." "Whalen Kendall married a woman named Hazel Schmid. Ring any bells?"

She shook her head.

"She had a daughter named Sophia."

Anna sat back in the chair. "I don't understand what you're saying," she said.

"Hazel left Whalen shortly after he came back from the First World War, and she returned to her family. As far as I know she never had contact with the Kendalls again. Their daughter was Sophia. Hazel remarried, a man named MacBride." Now recognition registered on her face. "So your mother was known as Sophia MacBride for most of her life, not Sophia Kendall. She got married in the forties," I said. "When was your oldest sibling born?"

"The twins, Mike and Nathan, were born in 1950. Mom was older when she started her family. Well, nowadays she wouldn't have been considered older, but for back then she was. I think all of us were born after she was thirty."

"Do you remember your grandmother? Hazel?"

"Oh, yes, she died…in '78, I think?" she said. "Yeah, because she was about eighty-four or eighty-five when she died. I mean, she'd always been old to me, since she was almost seventy when I was born."

"Anna, do you understand what I'm saying to you?"

She only smiled at me.

"You and your siblings are the heirs of Sandy Kendall. Your grandfather was not Tom MacBride. He was a step-grandfather. Your biological grandfather was Whalen Kendall," I said.

"I hear you," she said.

"I take it this is a surprise?"

"Very much so," she said.

"Then you can't help me," I said.

"Why not? What did you need to know?"

"I was hoping somebody could tell me why Hazel left Whalen, and if Hazel remembered the goings-on in that house," I said.

"You're right, I can't help you," she said. "I truly can't."

"Are you okay?"

"I'm a bit shell-shocked. Are you sure about all of this?"

"Not one hundred percent, because I haven't seen a birth record for Sophia yet, but I'm fairly certain."

"Well, none of it matters to me. The Kendalls were all long gone before I came into the picture," she said.

"I have to ask…why did you move to New Kassel? If you knew nothing about the Kendalls then, was it just a co-incidence?" I asked.

"Evidently so," she said. "Blake had a job at Wisteria General Hospital. We lived in Wisteria for a while, and then it got too commercial for Blake's taste, so we found a house here. I had no idea I'd been living a few blocks from where my real great-grandfather had lived. And his family."

Coincidences do happen, Mort had said.

"I might be able to get you some photographs," Anna said. "My oldest brother, Mike—even though he's a twin, he was born first, so he never lets us forget he's the oldest— he got most of my mom's old pictures. I remember him specifically saying a few years back that he didn't know who half of the people were in the pictures, but he just didn't have the heart to throw them away."

"That would be great," I said. "I could copy any that might be of interest."

"Sure," she said. "I'll drive down and get them next weekend."

"Where does he live?"

"Cape Girardeau," she said.

"I'd really appreciate that, Anna."

"Sure, whatever I can do to help," she said. "Why do you want to know all of this? I'm assuming it has something to do with the historical society."

"I'm buying the old Kendall house. Your grandfather's sister, Glory, was a fabric artist. She made the most amazing quilts," I said. "I'm going to set up the house as a textile museum."

"Why the interest in my grandmother? What has she got to do with it?"

"Well, as you know, all three of the siblings ended their lives in the house, and Hazel left just a short while before all of that happened. I thought maybe she could answer, or at least shed some light on, why they may have decided to end their lives. Maybe help me to understand just what went on," I said. "Not that I have to know these things to have the textile museum. I suppose it's more for my own personal interest. But since Glory Kendall will be the main focus of the display, it would help if I could shed some light on why she ended her life."

"I understand," she said. We talked a little more about family histories in general, and then she told me some animal stories from the veterinary hospital. Anna has always been very personable, and I like her a great deal. Her cat had even snuggled up next to me and started purring. A victory, according to Anna.

"I gotta go, it's late," I finally said.

"I'll let you know when I get the pictures from my brother," she said. "And I'm sure I'll hear about the museum when it opens. I'd like to be one of the first to see everything."

"I'll give you and your family a private tour," I said, and smiled. "You sure you're okay with this?"

"Fine," she said. "Just a little surprised. I've never really taken much interest in the past, so it doesn't have the impact on me as it would, say, somebody like yourself."

"Fair enough," I said, and left Anna's house.

On the way back home I dialed Sheriff Mort to see how Maddie Fulton was. I got a recording and left a message.

Well. Eight hours of tracking down Anna Gatewood only to come up completely empty-handed. It was clear that Anna had never heard any family stories about the Kendalls, and so I doubted any of her siblings had, either. In fact, I was beginning to doubt that even Sophia had known anything. She'd probably just been told that her father had died and that was it. According to the newspaper article, she was only an infant when Hazel left with her. All my sleuthing had been a total waste of time.

THIRTEEN

THE NEXT DAY WAS SATURDAY, and the rose show was a week away. My local rose expert was in the hospital, and Eleanore was in jail. I supposed everything would fall to Tobias. He is the one I would trust to carry on everything in Maddie's absence. My work, for the most part, was finished. All I had to do was show up and be there for emergencies and make sure all of the refreshment stands were stocked. The shop owners would take care of their own shops, so I didn't have to worry about them. They look forward to events like the rose show, which bring amazing numbers of people to town, people who eat at our restaurants and shop at our stores.

I sat on my back patio, drinking a cup of chai and watching the birds flutter around the mimosa tree. When Rudy and I picked out the location to build this house, I saw this mimosa tree off in the distance from the road. My Grandma Keith had always had two mimosa trees on her farm, and as a kid, I thought they were the most exotic things I'd ever seen. When you think about it, they don't look like the run-of-the-mill trees you see in Missouri, with their fluffy pink flowers and tiny leaves. So I asked the contractor if there was any way he could leave the mimosa tree if we built a house here, and he said yes. That was what settled it.

Well, that and the fact that Rudy had plenty of room to drive golf balls without breaking any windows. Rudy didn't even play golf yet. He said he needed to practice at home for a few years before he ever stepped foot on a range.

I heard the phone ring inside the house, and Rudy came out and handed me the handset. He kissed me on top of the head and said, "Matthew had breakfast. He just needs to get dressed."

"All right," I said. Then I answered the phone. It was Mort.

"Just wanted to let you know that Maddie Fulton is awake and asking to see you," he said.

Relief flooded me. "Oh, thank goodness she's all right," I said.

"She's been awake since last night, but they didn't want her to have any visitors except her closest family," he said.

"Oh, sure, I totally understand that," I said. "I'll stop by on my way to work."

"You work seven days a week?" he asked.

"Sometimes. You know, the weekend is the busiest time in a town like this."

"I see," he said. "I also wanted to let you know that Eleanore is being released."

"No charges?"

"Maddie said she didn't want to press any trespassing charges, and there was nothing else to charge Eleanore with," he said.

"Not even attempted murder?" I asked.

Mort chuckled.

"Can't you charge her with something?" I said. "She needs a few more days in jail."

"Maddie thinks it was an accident, and she's probably

right," he said. "However, Eleanore will be unbearable to live with, since now she's convinced she was a victim of...well, I'm not sure exactly. She wants to bring charges against the sheriff's department for harassment."

"Oh, great," I said.

"Yeah. Can I ask you something?"

"What?"

"What spaceship did she get off of?" he said.

"We've been trying to figure that out for a long time."

He laughed, and we hung up. I finished my chai and went inside to get Matthew dressed. The girls had spent the night with the anime club, and Rudy was just getting ready to leave. He needed to check on a display at a store he'd finished last week. I kissed him and then swiped at a small speck of shaving gel. "Your face is soft," I said.

He ran a finger across my jaw and then winked at me. "I'm cooking tonight," he said on the way out the door.

"What are you cooking?"

"It's a surprise."

"Okay," I said and looked at Matthew. "What do you think it's gonna be?"

"Macaroni and cheese," he said.

"Probably."

Matthew and I drove out to Wisteria General and made our way to the intensive care floor, after having stopped by Maddie's house to gather a bouquet of roses from her garden. The nurses would not allow Matthew into the room, so I left him sitting with the desk nurse under penalty of death if he misbehaved or broke anything. Of course, I then had to be more specific. "That means don't leave this chair. Don't touch anything. You can talk to the nice lady, that's it."

He stuck out his lower lip and crossed his arms.

I entered Maddie's room, almost as if walking on egg-shells. I was a bit apprehensive about what sort of condition she would be in. Her head was propped up slightly, and she still had IVs and tubes everywhere. She looked like hell, but I wasn't going to say that.

"So," she said. "I really do look as bad as I feel."

"I didn't say anything," I said.

"Your expression says it all," she said, and smiled. "Actually, I feel really lucky and happy and exhilarated. I'm alive. And you brought me roses!"

I smiled and handed them to her.

"And they're my roses," she said, breathing their scent in deeply. Then she added, "I know that whole exhilarated part is hard to believe, but it's true."

This time I laughed. "You scared us," I said.

"I scared myself. Look, Torie," she said, reaching out with one hand. I took her hand in mine and she squeezed. "I can never thank you enough."

"All I did was show up unannounced," I said. "Everybody else cusses me out for that."

"You acted quickly," she said. "That and coincidence saved me."

"It really was just my nosy nature that saved you. I didn't want to wait until the next day to find out what you were going to tell me."

"Well, see there? Don't ever be ashamed of who you are, then. It saved my life."

"Maddie, do you have any idea how this happened?" I asked.

"Who knows," she said. "Strychnine is used in lots of

things. You know, they used to use it for medicinal purposes way back when."

"The doctor said you got a very small dose," I said.

"Yeah, so I think I just got into something…you know, in the garage or something. I don't specifically remember anything that could have had strychnine in it, but who really knows."

"Well, I'm glad you're back with us," I said.

"Listen, Torie, what I wanted to tell you was about Glory Kendall."

"What about her?"

"The other night when I was getting Glory's quilt top ready to give to you for the display, I kept thinking about my grandma, trying to remember anything she might have said about the Kendall family. My grandmother was one of Glory's best and only friends. She said Glory was lonely, I remember that. The girl only had a handful of friends, and she pretty much was not allowed out of the house. I mean, she went out some, but I got the feeling that Glory just didn't go anywhere very often. Grandma said she almost always went to Glory's house to visit, not the other way around."

"Why the tight reins on Glory?"

"My grandma said that Glory had a lover. Young man who lived in Wisteria, I think, or somewhere close by. When her father and brothers found out, they forbade her to see him, and she just never went many places after that. Now, this is all secondhand and coming through the interpretation of my grandma, so take it with a grain of salt."

Maddie's breathing seemed more labored, so I didn't want to stay much longer. Her eyes had dark, purple shadows beneath them. It looked as though even blinking was difficult. "When do you get to go home?"

"They won't say. I'm thinking a week, maybe sooner if I start flirting with the doctor," she said, and winked.

"Look, Maddie, I know you're tired, and my son probably has the nurse tied up by now, so I'm going to head out," I said. "I'll come by again tomorrow."

"Thank you so much for the roses," she said. "I came close to never smelling a rose again."

"You're welcome," I said. "Hope you don't mind that I cut them from your bushes."

"That's what they're for," she said.

As I was headed out the door, a man about Maddie's age came in with a bright yellow get well balloon and a box of chocolates. "This is my brother, Kevin," she said.

"Nice to meet you," I said, then turned to leave.

"Oh, Torie, one more thing," she said.

"Yeah?"

"One other thing I do remember my grandmother saying, and I remember it because she said it more than once. In fact, she said it pretty much every time the Kendall family came up. She used to say that she couldn't stand the oldest brother. I can't remember his name…"

"Whalen?"

"Yes, Whalen. She said he was a no-account. Whatever a no-account is. She really didn't like that man," she said.

"Thanks a bunch, Maddie. I'll see you later."

When I went out to the nurse's station to retrieve my son, the nurse looked both entertained and irritated. My son will talk a person's leg off. Whenever he gets around people that are not his two sisters, I think, he realizes that this is his chance to say everything he's ever wanted to say, and so he just dumps sentence after sentence with incredible determination. He will talk over people. He'll even talk while two other people are talking, all the while thinking he's part of the conversation, even though what he's talking about has nothing to do with what they're talking about. So the nurse looked quite overwhelmed, as though her circuits were on overload and if she heard one more word her brain would fry. At the same time, she was smiling. He is cute, after all. Of course, he can only ride on his looks for so long.

I thanked the desk nurse for watching Matthew, and we left.

THE WORK WEEK had gone by fairly quickly. Maddie continued to get stronger and the majority of my time had been taken up by Rachel's play. If I wasn't running to the school with items to use as props, I was taking food to the cast members. Now, I'm not a good cook, mind you, but all the kids sung my praises when I showed up with homemade mostaccioli. They're high school kids, what do you expect?

I had gone to Marty Tarullo's house on Wednesday but nobody was home. So I thought I'd try again today. I pulled up at my mother's house and went inside to drop Matthew off with her. Her house smelled so good, I could have started eating the first thing I found. She was making her homemade vegetable soup.

I kissed Matthew goodbye, and then Colin came running down the hallway with one shoe on and one shoe in his hand. "Wait, wait, wait," he said.

"What?"

"I'm going with you."

"Going where?" I said. "Colin, I'm going to work."

My mother gave me her best *read my mind* look, but I couldn't for the life of me read her mind. All I managed to accomplish was to realize that she was trying to silently tell me something, and that got me even more confused. "Where are you going to work?" he asked.

"The Gaheimer House," I said. "Where I always work."

His shoulders slumped. "When I was sheriff, you rarely ever worked at your office. You were always out in cemeteries and stuffy old courthouses and...places."

I gaped at him.

"You mean to tell me you're not going *anywhere* today other than the Gaheimer House?" he asked, clearly irritated.

I glanced at my mother, who nodded her head, albeit casually.

"Uh...well, I was going to meet with a man named Marty Tarullo, since I was going to be in Wisteria already. He lives here. Then...I was going to go by the Kendall house. There's something I wanted to...check out. Colin, why do you care?"

"Hang on one second," he said. He ran back down the hallway with his shoe in his hand.

When he was out of earshot, my mother took the opportunity to finally talk. "Torie, please let him go with you," she said. "He's driving me crazy. He wants to do something so badly. He is going stir-crazy with this new job. He keeps reaching for his holster, but he doesn't wear one anymore! He listens to the police radio. All night! If I'd known he would be this miserable being mayor..."

"Is he really that miserable being mayor, or is it that he's more miserable not being sheriff?"

"Whichever. Please, Torie. For your poor, handicapped mother, please take my husband with you!"

"Well, well," I said, crossing my arms.

"This is not funny," she said. "I'll bake you a pie."

"A pie? You think putting up with Colin all day is worth a measly pie?"

"Hey, I already babysit your son, isn't that worth something?"

"Yes, but I pay you for that!" I said.

"Okay, two pies."

"No, Mom, there are no pies in the world worth having to put up with Colin. You don't understand," I said. "I just got to a point where I don't have to deal with him. I finally got a new sheriff in town, who actually likes me. He actually listens to me and considers my input."

"I'll bake you a homemade banana cake," she said.

"Oh, you're evil."

We stared at each other for a good thirty seconds.

"All right, it's a deal," I said.

Colin came back out wearing his sunglasses and a hat and both shoes this time. "All right, I'm ready," he said.

"Torie, are you sure it's all right if Colin tags along?" my mother said, smiling.

Banana cake. Remember I'm getting homemade banana cake. I can do this.

May as well start calling me Faust.

FOURTEEN

"So WHERE ARE WE HEADED?" Colin asked as we got in my car.

"A man named Marty Tarullo's house," I said. Last night I'd checked the white pages and found an address for him on Canon Avenue.

"And who is he?"

"He's a man who puts flowers on the grave of Glory Anne Kendall every June. Even though she's been dead for eighty-plus years."

"Why?"

"If I knew that I wouldn't be going to see him, now would I?" I said. I made a turn onto Wyatt Drive and then went down two streets and made a right. "I'm hoping he's not dead. The man has to be ancient, but Father Bingham said he saw him just last year."

Colin was quiet a moment, filling the space in my front seat with determined reflection. After a moment he spoke. "Who's Glory Anne Kendall?"

I rubbed my forehead and tried to fill him in best as I could before I pulled into Mr. Tarullo's driveway. I only had a few short minutes, because Mr. Tarullo lived just eight or nine blocks from my mother and Colin.

The story-and-a-half white house was quaint, with a small front porch and a round window where the attic should be. I love round windows—I suppose because they defy what "normal" windows are supposed to be. Maybe they remind me of Hobbit houses and windows. Or maybe they're just cute. At any rate, the window lent a certain charm to the house, and there was an enormous weeping willow tree in the front yard that sort of capped it all off. Along the sidewalk, somebody had painstakingly planted petunias or pansies; I'm not sure which. They both sort of look the same to me. I just knew that they were colorful and low to the ground.

I grabbed my purse and gave Colin last-minute instructions. "Listen, let me do the talking," I said.

He puffed his chest as if he were about to start beating it. I added, "Look, you're not the sheriff anymore, you're not in uniform, and you're kinda big and scary, so if you go in there being all aggressive, you're liable to freak him out. Me, I'm little and unassuming. So let me do this."

Colin chuckled a bit, most likely because of my "little and unassuming" remark. I just glared at him.

"Right," he said after a few moments.

I rang the doorbell, and the door was answered by a woman who looked to be in her late fifties or sixties. Her hair color came from a bottle—it had sort of a pinkish tint to it, and last I checked, that particular hue didn't appear in nature. "Yes?" she said.

"Hi, I'm Torie O'Shea, the historian over in New Kassel. Father Bingham at the Catholic church told me that Mr. Tarullo could most likely help me on a matter that happened almost eighty years ago. Is Mr. Tarullo home so that I could speak with him?"

"Dad's out back in the garden," she said.

"In the garden?" I asked.

"Fell and broke his hip three years ago pulling weeds. Can't get that man to listen to nobody," she said. She stepped outside onto the porch and then down the steps to lead us around to the backyard. "I keep telling him, 'Dad, you're ninety-four years old. You need to let one of your grandkids pull the weeds.' But he won't listen. Then again, maybe he's lived this long by doing all of his own yard work. My grandpa worked every day until he was eighty-nine. Three days after he decided to stop working, he dropped dead. So maybe Dad has the right idea," she said.

"Well, maybe," I said, smiling at her.

She opened the gate to the backyard and sure enough, there was an old man, bent way over his walker, tugging on some stupid weed that was encroaching on his tomato plants. The vegetable garden was pretty big, I'd say twenty feet by thirty feet, and along the fence there were several rows of what looked like blackberries or raspberries. I used to help my grandma pick berries when I was a kid. I always ate more than I put in the bucket.

"Dad, there are people here to see you from New Kassel," the woman said. "A historian who wants to ask you some questions. Father Bingham sent them."

Marty Tarullo either didn't hear her or didn't care. His daughter smiled at me while waiting for her father to acknowledge our presence. "Oh, I'm Connie," she said.

I shook her hand. "This is my stepfather, Colin Brooke."

"Oh," she said. "Ex-sheriff Brooke? How's the new job?"

"Different," he said.

"I like the new sheriff," she said. "He seems good for the community."

Colin smiled at her, but I could have sworn I heard his teeth grinding in the process.

Marty Tarullo stood up then. It seemed to take him a whole two minutes just to straighten his back. He moved his walker around and came toward us.

"Dad?" Her voice got a notch louder. "I said, there are two people here—"

"I heard you," he said. He waved at Colin and me and then motioned to several Adirondack chairs on the back patio. "Have a seat."

"Would you all like something to drink?" Connie asked.

"Water for me," I said.

"Any sort of soda," Colin said.

Connie disappeared to get the drinks. Marty wiped his forehead with a handkerchief he had stuffed in his back pocket. I'm often surprised by how good some people look considering they're nearly a century old, or how well they move. If I hadn't known my boss Sylvia was as old as dirt, I would not have been able to tell it. Marty Tarullo looked his age and moved like somebody whose joints had been rubbing together for a millennium.

"My daughter thinks I'm deaf," he said. "Can't taste nothing no more. Takes me forever to pee. Got hairs growing out my nose and ears. Don't look like myself no more. Oh, and I got two toes on my left foot that have no feeling. Can't figure out why. So, pretty much, nothing works right on this old body. Except my hearing. My hearing is fine. Can't seem to get that through her darned head."

I laughed. I couldn't help it. Mr. Tarullo winked at me then.

"Guess if I look like I'm deaf, she just thinks I'm deaf," he said. "It's something, you know? You let your kids live with you the first twenty years of their lives, then they let you live with them the last twenty of yours."

"So, this is your daughter's house?" I asked.

"Nah, it's mine. She got a divorce. Her husband met some young thing and left her. After twenty-two years. Hell, they were just getting to the good part. Anyway, so my wife and I told her she could come stay here. That was eighteen years ago. My wife passed about eight years ago. Anyway, other than the fact she thinks I'm deaf and I'm too old to pull weeds, we get along fine."

"Does she have any children?"

"Two," he said. "Now she has two grandkids. They sure as fire light up the place."

I smiled. "So, Mister Tarullo," I said. "I'm here about—"

"You're here about Glory Kendall. I know why you're here."

"How could you know that?" I asked and glanced at Colin.

"Don't really know anybody in New Kassel except Father Bingham, and I only know him because of Glory Kendall. So that has to be why you're here," he said. "Somebody finally looking into that whole mess?"

"Well, not in any official capacity, no. As a historian I'm investigating because I'm buying the Kendall house and I want to turn it into a textile museum. For quilts."

"Glory's quilts?" he asked.

"Yes," I said. "Hers and those made by other historical women of the area."

"You want to know why I put flowers on her grave every year, don'tcha?"

"That would be a good place to start," I said and smiled.

Marty Tarullo was quiet a moment, looking off at his

garden. "I can still see her plain as day. I was about nine or ten years old the day she came to the house and told my brother that she couldn't marry him. She'd come around in one of those fancy cars her brother Whalen had been driving. There were only a handful of people in the whole county who had a motorcar that early, but they were bankers, so everybody just assumed they would be the ones to get the first car. Anyway, Whalen brought her around in the car. I could tell Glory had been crying. Those big blue eyes of hers were swollen, and her nose was red. But she put on a good show. I was half in love with her myself. She was so beautiful."

"Why did she call off the engagement?"

His eyes peered at me sharply. "You want her reason or the real reason?"

"Both," Colin said before I could.

Connie came out then and put our refreshments on the table. "You okay, Dad?" she asked.

"Yeah," he said and waved a hand.

After Connie had gone back in and shut the door, he continued. "Glory wouldn't even come in the house. She stood on the porch. I'd answered the door. She was wearing her hat with the feathers and a long yellow dress. I can still see her standing there. Anyway, she asked me to go get Anthony, my brother. So I went and got him. Then I stood behind him in the doorway. She said, 'I can't marry you, Tony. I'm not ready for it. Rupert still needs me.' My brother told her that he could wait. He loved her, he was in no hurry, and he understood that Rupert came first right now, he said." He paused then.

"Did you ever meet Rupert?" I asked.

He nodded. "Rupe was in bad shape. He was all messed up from those trenches. Only thing that got him through it was Glory's letters. Then, he told me once, he got home only to find that evil lurked in tiny towns as much as it did in the trenches."

I glanced at Colin, who shifted in his chair. "Do you know what he meant by that?" Colin asked.

He made a dismissive gesture with his hands. "Nothing I can prove, only speculation. Anyway, so Tony understood about Rupe, and he knew Glory could never leave her brother until he was better. So Tony, being Tony, said that when they got married, Rupert could move in with them. Not only was my brother madly in love with Glory and woulda done anything for her, but he was very thoughtful of others, you see. So it made sense to me that he'd offer his house to Rupert. Glory said to him, 'I can't do it. I just can't be married.' Then she glanced over her shoulder to where Whalen was sitting in that car. I didn't catch it at the time, 'cause I was too young, but now I understand a little more. Glory was scared. Whalen was making her say all this. So Tony said to her, 'You mean not ever? You can't get married ever?' And she hung her head and said, 'Not ever. It's over.'"

It was quiet in Mr. Tarullo's backyard, except for the birds playing in his birdbath.

"My brother got upset then, you see. Last time he'd seen Glory, everything was fine. Now all of a sudden she's telling him she can't be with him at all. So he said, 'It's because I'm Italian, isn't it?'"

"Because he was Italian?" I said. "Are you for real?"

"Back then, the Irish, the Chinese, the Italians...we

were all like contaminated goods. The Americans who'd come over on the *Mayflower* and such, they'd been here hundreds of years, and they didn't trust us. We were dark. We were Catholic, we didn't speak the greatest English— if we spoke it at all—and for the most part, we tended to stay to ourselves in little communities inside big cities, like ghettos, because the average immigrants were so poor they couldn't buy a farm or move to a richer part of town. My family, well, we were a little better off than some, because my father had been fairly upper class back in Italy. So we had the money to bypass that whole ghetto, you see. But when we moved here to Granite County, everybody whispered about us."

He spoke the truth. I knew he did. The Irish had been just as mistrusted, if not more, because their numbers were so high and they had a large number of unchaperoned or unaccompanied women who immigrated. People felt as though that was trouble waiting to happen, and sometimes it did. At the turn of the century, established American families thought the new male immigrants would take all their jobs and their daughters. I knew this about our immigrant history, but unless I witness it firsthand, I often forget about it. Until Marty spoke the words, it never would have occurred to me that Glory would not have been able to marry Anthony Tarullo because he was Italian.

"Tony told me later that Whalen had said more than once that he wasn't good enough for Glory and that it would cause a scandal in New Kassel. Whalen told Glory that if she married Tony, they couldn't stay in the county. They'd have to move, or else her marriage would force Whalen and her father to leave town."

"What did her father have to say about the match?" Colin asked.

"I don't think he was thrilled with it," Mr. Tarullo said, "but he was allowing the marriage, and Tony said that Mr. Kendall had even offered him a job at the bank."

"Wow," I said. "So it was Whalen who was opposed, not Sandy."

"I think her father woulda been happy if she'd found somebody else, but he was going to make the best of it if that's what Glory wanted," Mr. Tarullo said.

"So you think the real reason she called off the wedding was because Tony was Italian?" I asked.

"I think the real reason was because of Whalen. I think she was scared of him," Mr. Tarullo said. "And I think she'da done whatever he said for her to do."

"Why?" Colin asked.

I knew the answer before Marty Tarullo said it. "Rupert. He threatened Glory with Rupert."

"I think so," Mr. Tarullo said, "but I can't prove it."

"But why?" I asked.

"Well, that would be the sixty-four-thousand-dollar question, now, wouldn't it?"

"You think it's just because Tony was Italian?"

"I think Whalen hated Tony and he was gonna get his way or else," Mr. Tarullo said.

I took a drink of water and watched a big white fluffy cloud float across the sky. "Wow," I said.

"So...as to the reason I go to Glory's grave every year," Mr. Tarullo said. "Time went by. Rupert hung himself from the tree in their backyard. Now, if Glory hadda been telling the truth and she couldn't marry Tony because of Rupert, then…there wouldn't be nothing stopping her now, would there? So me and my brother, we went to the funeral. I'll never forget this as long as I live. My brother got Glory off to herself, and I was standing guard. Tony said, 'You cough real loud if you see Whalen or Mr. Kendall coming.' So I did, I stood there at the edge of the wall in the hallway. I tried not to listen or watch them, but it was hard. Once I snuck a peek—my brother had just kissed her, and then Glory cried in his arms. Whalen came storming down the hall, and I coughed, and Glory ran up the stairs and Tony came around the corner as if he'd just been to the washroom or something. There was a big stained-glass window in the hall, and Whalen…Well, he never said nothing. Not one word. He just picked Tony up and threw him through that window. Glass went everywhere, and I stood frozen to the spot. Then Whalen walked by me and rapped his knuckles on my head. Tony and I left then. My brother was all cut up and bleeding. He had a scar on his arm until the day he died from that—but no matter. It was the last time either of us saw Glory alive."

"What happened next?" Colin said. "You can't just leave us there."

"Seven months later, she was dead," he said. "Even though my brother knew he wouldn't get to marry Glory, he still loved her. In fact, he loved her until the day he died, back in 1982. He used to take flowers to her grave on the anniversary of her death. Then one day after his first heart attack, he asked me if I'd take over doing it for him when he couldn't do it anymore. I said of course I would. I loved Glory, too. She was so kind. I had trouble with numbers when I was a kid, and Glory would help me with my division."

"So you take flowers to her grave every year for your brother," I said. I had to swipe at a tear that had formed in the corner of my eye. The story was heartbreaking. His brother's devotion was…so romantic.

"Yeah," he said. "Not sure how much longer I can do it."

"Let me test my understanding," Colin said. "Whalen threw Tony out of the house, through a stained-glass window…and nobody did anything about it?"

Mr. Tarullo gave a chuckle. "Whalen was a banker. Prominent citizen. Nobody even questioned it, other than in the private circles of the gossip queens."

"What did the gossip queens have to say?" I asked.

"They said that Tony got Glory pregnant. That's why Whalen hated him. When the Kendalls forbade the marriage, Glory killed herself rather than have to be an unwed mother," he said. "All horseshit, if you ask me."

"Why's that?" I asked.

"Well, if she was pregnant, she'd've been just about ready to give birth when she killed herself, and she didn't look pregnant. I mean, I didn't see her alive, but none of her friends or family mentioned it. There was no gossip about it until after she killed herself. At her funeral, she did not look pregnant. I know, because I was there. Plus, I can't believe Glory woulda killed her baby, and that's exactly what she woulda done if she'd killed herself and had been pregnant at the time. Besides, Sandy Kendall had enough money, he could have sent her away, like rich people sometimes did. She coulda had the baby somewhere else and come back like nothing had ever happened. Rupert was gone by then, it's not like Sandy was afraid to send her away for Rupe's sake. The whole thing don't make no sense."

"Understatement of the year," I said.

"There's one other thing," he said, "then I'm finished with this whole subject."

Colin smiled at me, and I said, "What's that?"

"I think she was murdered."

"Oh, boy," Colin muttered.

"Why?" I said.

"She never took laudanum."

"Yes, but she was distraught. First she had to call off her engagement to a man I think she clearly loved, then her brother committed suicide. Maybe a doctor prescribed it to help her sleep. Just because she didn't use it before doesn't mean she didn't start using it," I said.

"See, this is the part I can't prove," he said.

"Why's that?"

"Because the people involved are dead. But the next-door neighbor, Doris, she said that Sandy Kendall had come over to borrow her laudanum the night before."

"So Glory asked for the laudanum, her father borrowed the neighbor's, and then Glory overdosed on it. If anything, it sounds more like an accident than a suicide."

"Except when Doris went over the next day to see how Glory was feeling, Sandy and Whalen let her into the house and told her that there'd been a terrible incident. That Glory had taken the whole bottle of laudanum. When Doris raced up the steps to Glory's room, she was lying there dead, all right, but she wasn't lying there all peaceful-like. Like one would expect from laudanum. No, her back was arched and her face was all in a grimace. Doris said she ran scream-ing from the room and couldn't close her eyes for weeks without seeing Glory like that."

The bottom fell out of my stomach. Colin and I looked at each other. "Strychnine," I whispered.

"That's right, that's what I said. Sandy told Doris—according to Doris—that he'd pay off all her debts if she wouldn't tell the authorities or the papers about what she'd saw. He didn't want people to think of his daughter looking like that. He wanted people to remember her being all sweet and beautiful, like she was."

"But what about the authorities? Surely they would have understood as soon as they saw the body," I said.

"Yeah, which is why I say they didn't call the authorities until a day or two later, when the stiffness had settled and she looked fairly normal again."

I sat back, speechless.

"What about this Doris?" Colin asked. "How come she told you all of this?"

"Because I married her daughter," Mr. Tarullo said. "One day we got to talking and she just confessed all of it. It's a good thing she didn't tell me or my brother right after Glory's death, because my brother would have killed Whalen Kendall himself."

"Why?"

"Because nobody would think for a second that Sandy killed Glory. It was Whalen, I'll betcha. And Tony woulda killed him, and then my brother woulda went to jail. So I'm glad the son-of-a-bitch got a conscience finally and blew his brains out. He was a complete no-account."

I'd been listening to Mr. Tarullo speak, but I'd only half heard everything he'd said since he'd described the state of Glory Kendall's body. I'd been flashing back to what Maddie Fulton had looked like when I found her, which led me to the obvious question: How much of a coincidence is it that—if Mr. Tarullo is correct—Glory Anne Kendall was killed with strychnine and then, almost eighty-five years later, Maddie Fulton comes down sick with strychnine poisoning? The only connection was the quilts.

"Mr. Tarullo, I can't thank you enough for speaking to us so frankly about all of this."

"I've been waiting all these years to tell somebody," he said. "Nobody really cared before."

"I hate to just leave, but something very urgent has just come to my attention," I said, "so Colin and I have to go. Thank your daughter for her hospitality."

"I sure will," he said. "Take care."

I tapped Colin on the shoulder and all but ran out of the backyard to my car.

"You thinking what I'm thinking?" Colin asked. Funny, I was nearly running, but with his long legs he was walking normally.

"Worse," I said as we got in the car.

"What's the connection between Maddie's strychnine poisoning and Glory's? There has to be one, I can see it on your face," he said.

"Get out your cell phone and call Sheriff Mort," I said. "The night that Maddie got sick, she'd been preparing a quilt that Glory had made."

"So?" he said, dialing.

"I remember her saying the first time we talked about her quilts that one of them still had pins in it. It was spread out on her guest bed. And there were straight pins on the nightstand. I think those pins had been coated with strychnine," I said. "Meant for Glory, which she obviously found.

The thing is, if the person who coated the pins with strychnine in the first place—Whalen—then killed himself without telling anybody how he poisoned her…then those same poisoned pins would still have been in the quilt basting the three sections together."

"Mort, it's Colin," he said into the cell phone. "You need to get a unit over to Maddie Fulton's house as soon as possible."

He explained to Mort everything I'd just said as we drove at top speed to Maddie's house.

FIFTEEN

"IT MAKES TOTAL SENSE NOW," I said. "Well, some of it does. Well, certain parts of it do." I took the Hollyberry Falls turn about ten miles an hour too fast. Colin gripped the door handle.

"You're speeding."

"Yeah, and you're not the sheriff anymore," I said, and chuckled.

"You're enjoying this, aren't you?"

"What?"

"Me not being the sheriff."

"Oh, *hell* yes."

"Okay, so what makes sense now?"

"I remember Father Bingham saying that Father O'Brien told him that Sandy Kendall got special dispensation to have his daughter buried in the Catholic cemetery even though she'd committed suicide."

"So?"

"I'm thinking Sandy Kendall went to Father O'Brien, or whoever the pastor was at the time, and told him the truth. In confession. I think he went to the priest and said he knew for a fact his daughter had not committed suicide because his son had killed her and he wanted Glory buried in the family plot. It would completely explain how and why he got that accomplished," I said.

"If he knew his son, Whalen, had killed Glory... He confessed it to a priest but said nothing to the authorities?"

"It's his son," I said. "He'd already lost two out of three kids. I guess he couldn't bear to lose his third and last child."

Colin shrugged.

"This is all speculation. Without Father O'Brien coming back from the dead and breaking the oath of secrecy, I'll never know for sure, but it totally makes sense," I said.

"So you believe without a doubt that Whalen killed his sister," he said. "How are you gonna prove it?"

"I can't prove it. I don't need to prove it."

"What do you mean you don't need to prove it?"

I pulled the car in at Maddie Fulton's house just behind the squad car. Then I looked at Colin. "There's nobody to arrest," I said. "There's nobody in imminent danger, just as soon as we take care of these pins. Oh, speaking of which, I'll need the crime scene unit to take all of the sewing notions at the Gaheimer House that Geena and I removed from the Kendall house. Those could well be contaminated, too."

"All right, but why don't you need to prove this?"

"I'm not writing or publishing a dissertation on what happened. Nobody's being arrested. I'll know in my heart what happened, and that's good enough for me," I said.

"But what about the museum? Are you gonna tell tourists your speculation without proof?"

I thought about that for a minute. "Maybe."

He started to protest. Loudly.

"I can state up front that it's all speculation," I said.

"Don't bother," he said with his hands up. "If you're not going to do it right, then don't do it. If you can't prove Whalen poisoned his sister, then don't mention it. You just leave it as a mystery for the tourists to conclude what they will."

"Look, you can't tell me what to do with my own museum," I said.

"Well, I just did," he said, and got out of the car.

"Colin!" I said, following him. "I can state the facts that I have, the speculation that I've heard…"

"And you'll be doing no good for that family. Think about it, Torie. What has that poor family had to endure? Even dead. Beyond the grave, their names are still being thrown around in mockery. People joke about them, make fun of them. Now you're going to help people slander them? What if Whalen was completely innocent? What if Sandy Kendall poisoned his own daughter?"

"Why would he?" I asked.

"Why would Whalen? That's not the point," he said. "The point is, as of right now, you have a ninety-four-year-old man who remembers a few incidents from his child-hood, looking through half-love-crazy eyes. Sandy Kendall is as much a viable suspect as Whalen. So unless you can prove it, I suggest you not mention it."

"There is no banana cake worth having to put up with you!" I screeched.

"What?"

"Nothing." I stormed past him into Maddie's house, where I found Deputy Oldham and a crime scene investigator. "Hi, Deputy."

"Torie," she said. Deputy Wendy Oldham is new to the Granite County Sheriff's Department. She's about twenty-eight, with a touch of copper in her blond hair, and green eyes. I like Deputy Oldham a lot. In fact, ten years ago, when she was working her way through college, I used to pay her to do the landscaping for the Gaheimer House. Well, Sylvia actually paid her, but I hired her. "You said there's strychnine on some sewing pins?" She said that with pure disbelief in her voice, and I couldn't say that I blamed her.

"Yeah," I said. "Back here in the guest bedroom. Also, I'm assuming the poison has probably seeped into the surrounding fabric wherever there had been a pin. Maybe not, hell, I don't know. So I'd say take the whole quilt and the pins, and don't touch anything without gloves."

"Right," she said.

"Also, I've got some sewing notions at the Gaheimer House that may be contaminated." Then I thought about the morning glory quilt still in the frame. "And another quilt that's still basted in a frame. That needs to be checked, too."

"All right," she said. "We'll take care of it."

Then I opened my cell phone and called the Gaheimer House. Stephanie answered on the second ring.

"Stephanie, it's me. Don't touch the morning glory quilt that's still in the frame or any of the sewing notions."

"All right," she said.

"Don't let Geena touch them, either, if she's there."

"I won't," she said. "Why not?"

"I'll explain when I get there."

I really wanted to drop Colin off at his house, but that would mean driving all the way back out to Wisteria, so I dropped him off at his office, whether he wanted me to or not. "Hey," I said as he got out of my car. "Why don't we do a barbecue fund-raiser so that you can give this building a face-lift?"

He glanced at the tan rectangular building that served as city hall and his office, and back at me. "It is pretty stinkin' ugly, isn't it?"

"I thought I just didn't like the building because Bill was mayor, but now that you're mayor, I find I still don't like the building."

"Me, neither," he said. "All right, organize it. Let me know what you need me to do."

That's the great thing about New Kassel. Rarely do we ever tax anybody for anything. We just happily go about having fund-raisers, bazaars, and festivals. Speaking of which, the first day of the first annual rose show was fast approaching.

I drove back to my office at the Gaheimer House, grabbed a Dr Pepper, and drank half of the can standing in the kitchen. My sister came in and hauled out the chocolate chip cookies. "You look like you could use some chocolate chips," she said.

I ate one and chewed in silence. "You ever feel like... you're just going around in circles? Like you're doing what you think you should be doing rather than what you are supposed to be doing?"

"Rough day?" she asked.

"Yeah," I said. "Maybe it's just that when I think I've discovered the limits of what a human being can do to another human being, something else comes along that makes me realize how naive I've been all along."

"My dog puked on me today," Stephanie said.

"Oh, that blows," I said.

"What's the deal with the quilts?" she asked. She pulled out a chair and sat down.

I explained to her everything I'd learned. Then I told her about the fight I'd had with Colin.

"Not to be taking sides or anything, but what if he's right?" Stephanie asked. "What if Whalen was behaving the way he was because he was scared, too? I mean, you said yourself that Whalen's wife and daughter took off and never came back. There had to be a reason for that."

"I know," I said, "but a few people have told me that they didn't trust Whalen or they thought he was no good. Not just one person."

She shrugged. "Well, you can never tell."

"You really can't, can you?" I said. "I'm going home. The rose show opens in a week, and I'm hoping that Tobias has gotten the list of roses from Maddie and that everything is in order."

"You hope?" she asked, laughing.

"I know, not a very good attitude to have," I said. "Trust me, it's a first. I'm usually overinvolved in the festivals."

"Don't make it a habit," she said. I held up my half-empty Dr Pepper can, noiselessly asking if she wanted to finish it. She took it and drank the rest as I walked out of the Gaheimer House to my car.

After dinner, I decided I wanted to talk with Sheriff Mort, so I called the office. He wasn't there. Peg said he'd gone fishing and was off all weekend, which meant I'd have to wait until Monday to even ask him what I wanted to ask him. Not to mention Peg said that something urgent had come up on one of his cases and she needed to talk to him before the weekend was out. Even though she had tried his cell phone, I called it anyway. He didn't answer. So I called

Colin at home. He would know where to find Mort, because if it had anything to do with fishing, Colin knew about it.

"Hey, it's Torie," I said when he answered. "I'm trying to get ahold of Mort, but he's not answering his cell phone."

"So?" he said. "I'm not his keeper."

"No, I know, but he went fishing. Where's a good place to go fishing around here?"

"You called a man on his cell phone while he was fishing?" he asked.

"Yes. Now where would he have gone?"

"Torie, you don't call a man's cell phone when he's fishing. My God, don't you know anything?"

He was truly appalled by my lack of fishing etiquette.

"Great, now I know. So where would he have gone?"

"Depends on what he's fishing for."

"Fish," I said. That was possibly the stupidest question I ever heard. "You know, with scales and gills and fins."

"What *kind* of fish, you dip."

"Uh…the wet kind."

He hung up on me.

I couldn't believe he actually hung up on me.

I called him back.

"I am not telling you where that man went fishing, because you'll just go out there and interrupt him," he said.

"Yes, that's the point. I have something very important I want to discuss with him," I said.

"No," he said.

"If you don't tell me, I'm just going to keep calling back," I said.

"You're horrible," he said. "Just so you know."

"I know, I know," I admitted.

"Mort likes to get catfish and bass. Everybody knows Hawk Point is the best place for that. Besides, he owns a little cabin on Hawk Point. About ten miles off the main road. And do not tell him I told you. He'll never trust me again if you do," he said.

It must be painful to be that cantankerous.

"I won't tell him. And just so you know, there's been a break on one of his cases and Peg needs to talk to him about it. I'm not just hunting him down for my own sake," I said. Although that was part of it. I'm honest.

I dropped Mary off at the skating rink in Wisteria because all of her girlfriends were going skating and she just *had* to go or she'd just *die*. The real reason was that Tony was going to be there. I could tell because she put an extra coating of lip gloss on, and now her lips looked liked she'd just eaten a side of bacon. I told her I'd pick her up at eleven. Next I went to Target for a super-duper can of bug spray, making sure it said DEET in huge bright letters. I guess I thought the brighter and bigger the letters were, the more DEET would be in the can. Then I headed out to Hawk Point.

Mort's cabin was a good ten miles off of the two-lane road that led into Hawk Point. It felt as though I'd just entered the wilderness. I couldn't even see a telephone or power line anywhere. When I got to the cabin, I doused myself in the bug spray, holding my breath and jumping around in the mist of chemicals. I took my cell phone and my keys but left my purse behind. No point in taking it with me. It's not like I'd need Gummy Bears and a checkbook to find the sheriff. It was almost dark, and there was a single light on in the run-down, grown-over cabin. Mort's gigantic new truck was parked in the front. I swear, I'd need a ladder just to get up in the thing.

I knocked on the door, but he didn't answer. That meant he was still out fishing. I wondered if he took a boat or a canoe like Colin usually did. If he did, all I could do was wait for him, because I wouldn't begin to know where he would be. I headed down to the water and walked along the edge, looking to see if I could find Mort anywhere or evidence of a boat. Like a dock. It occurred to me then that DEET wasn't going to help me with ticks, and my skin suddenly began to crawl. "Mort?" I called out.

I yelled his name a few more times and finally got a response. "Shhh," he said. "The fish are talking to me."

I whipped around and found him sitting on the bank about twenty feet away in the opposite direction from where I'd been looking. He was sitting on the ground. Right there smack dab in the middle of all the ticks and spiders and mosquitoes. He didn't even have a blanket.

"The fish are talking to you?" I said.

"Yes," he said. "Can't you hear them?"

"No, all I hear is the buzzing of the Amazon-sized mosquitoes that keep flying around my head," I said. "And whippoorwills. Which are kinda nice. And crickets. Which are really loud."

There was a *blurp* sound on the water. "See?" Mort said. "They're talking to me."

"Great," I said. "What are the fish saying?"

"They're saying, 'Tell that loudmouth who's come to see you that she's about ready to step on a snake.'"

"What?" I said. Mort looked up at me, and I realized what he'd just said. I started screaming and jumping around. My legs were going in directions they hadn't gone since sixth-grade gymnastics class. I didn't even know I could still bend that way. Mort hopped up, ran over, grabbed me by the collar, and yanked me off to the side as I saw something slither past me and into the water.

"Cottonmouth," he said. "Damned serious. Good thing it wasn't completely dark yet, or I wouldn't have seen it."

"Wonderful," I said, nearly fainting.

"What are you doing out here?" he asked.

"Well, Mr. Crocodile Dundee, if you'd answer your cell phone, I wouldn't have had to come out here," I said.

"What is it?"

"There's been a break on one of your cases, or some vital info of some sort, and Peg needs you to call in. I don't think she needs you to come in or anything. At least she didn't make it sound that way, but she does need to talk to you. And I know you're off for the next few days, but I also wanted to ask a favor of you," I said.

"What's that?"

"Would you reopen the file on the Kendall suicides?"

"Why?" he asked.

"I'd like it if you would just look over the evidence and see what the investigators at the time had picked up on," I said. "If you don't have time, if you could give the files to me and let me read them."

"You?"

"Or Colin. You know you can trust him," I said. I remembered what Colin had said and decided not to tell Mort the part about how I'd asked Colin where he was.

"What are you looking for?" he asked.

Something buzzed by my ear and I swiped at it furiously.

"Could we maybe go in the cabin or up to the cars? Somewhere away from this water?"

"Sure," he said. He walked me up to my car and stopped. I guessed he wasn't going to invite me in, and I figured he was going to head back down to his fishing as soon as I left. Colin had always said the best times to fish were at sunrise and sunset.

"I've got reason to believe that Glory Kendall may have been murdered," I said. I repeated what Marty Tarullo had told me. "I had Deputy Oldham take the pins and quilts into the lab for analysis."

"Good," he said. "Better safe than sorry."

"So, if she was actually murdered, the evidence that the investigators collected back in 1922 might suddenly mean something different," I said.

"All right," he said. "I'll get on it tomorrow."

I was speechless. That wasn't nearly as difficult as I'd thought it was going to be. I thought he was going to protest and whine and I'd have to convince him. "Oh," I said. "That was easy."

"I'll see you tomorrow," he said. "Thanks for coming down and giving me the message from Peg."

"Right," I said. "I'll be at the Gaheimer House for part of the day tomorrow. Then on to the rose show."

"Have a safe trip back," he said. Sure enough, he headed down to the water and his talking fish.

It was all a little anticlimactic.

SIXTEEN

I STOPPED BY MY MOTHER'S and stayed until it was time to pick up Mary from the skating rink. She showed me her latest painting, which was a really nice moody piece of an orange sunset and a girl carrying a water pail up to a silhouette of a church. I think it's awesome that she can pull an image from her mind and set it on canvas. Then it's there forever. Mom fed me some peach cobbler and I was on my way. I waited outside the skating rink for about twenty minutes as the kids all filed out of the building, laughing and giggling and talking all the way to their parents' cars.

All the kids except Mary.

After about ten more minutes, I went into the rink to see if I could find Mary maybe hanging around and talking to somebody, completely unaware of what time it was. Because that's Mary. Quite often I get upset with her over something, thinking that she was deliberately being disrespectful or negligent, when in fact she was just oblivious. I have no idea where her mind is most of the time, but it isn't in the here and now. Sounds like me, now that I think about it. Rudy gets upset with Mary a lot more than I do, and I think it's because I find it very difficult to get upset with a child who's behaving like me.

Mary wasn't in the skating rink, at least not that I could see. I checked the girls' restroom and, short of stomping into the boys' restroom, was at a loss as to where to look next. I ran back out to the parking lot to see if she was waiting for me in the car, but she wasn't. I went back into the skating rink and found a familiar face behind one of the skate rental counters. It was Helen's nephew. I couldn't remember his name at the moment, but I knew he knew who I was. "Hey, I dropped my daughter off here—"

"Rachel?"

"No, Mary. Have you seen her?"

"Oh, yeah, earlier in the evening," he said. "Haven't seen her in a while."

Okay, that panic that I can usually keep in check swelled right up in my throat, and I ran for the boys' restroom. Not to puke, but to see if she was hiding in there. God knows why she'd be hiding in there, but it was the only spot in the rink that I hadn't checked. She wasn't in the boys' room, however, and I had to apologize all over myself to the poor pimply-faced kid who had been taking a whiz. I think I made him pee on his shoe. I shoved the door to the bathroom open with the palm of my hand and kept on going, storming out of the rink. I flipped the cell phone and called Rudy.

"Is Mary at home?" I asked without saying hello.

"Torie?"

"Yes, it's your wife. Who else would be looking for Mary?"

"I'm confused."

"Is. Mary. At. Home? Simple enough question."

"No, she's at the skating rink," he said. "You don't have to be so hateful."

"No, she's not."

"What do you mean she's not?"

"She's not here."

"Well, where is she?"

"I don't know. That's why I'm calling."

"Oh, shit," he said.

"Has she called?"

"No," he said.

"Ask Rachel if she knows where Mary is."

I waited, scanning the parking lot, while Rudy asked Rachel if she knew the whereabouts of her very-much-in-trouble sister. "No, Rachel hasn't seen her."

My brain froze. I couldn't think. It didn't compute. She wasn't at home, she wasn't at the skating rink…I didn't know what to think next. Rachel had never done anything like this. How dare she be such a good kid. It had left me completely unprepared for Mary. Not that Mary was a bad kid—in fact, I'd say she was closer to normal and Rachel was the abnormal kid—but still…I'd never had to think this way. Where could she be?

She'd been kidnapped. That had to be it. What the hell else could it be? Hadn't I taught her never to go anywhere with strangers? Yes. Hadn't I taught her never to leave a party or an event with anybody other than her parents or grandparents? Yes. So then she had to have been taken. Right?

Wrong.

Just then a car pulled into the parking lot and out stepped Mary. I didn't recognize the driver of the car, who looked about twenty. Mary's friend Megan was in the backseat.

I flipped open my cell phone and hit redial. Rudy answered on half a ring. "Did you find her?" he asked.

"Yes, I found her."

"Is she all right?"

"For now," I said.

"Uh-oh," he said.

"Talk to you later."

I was storming across that parking lot without even realizing it.

"What in the hell do you think you're doing?" I screamed at her.

"Oh, hi, Mom."

"Don't you oh-hi-Mom me." I glanced at the driver. "Who the hell are you?"

"Uh…Zack," he said.

"Mom, this is Megan's brother," she said.

"Great. That's nice. Get your butt in my car now," I said. I didn't even look back at the car that had dropped off my daughter. I marched behind Mary across the parking lot.

When we got in the car, Mary was silent. She knew she was in trouble. I turned over the engine and headed straight for home.

Finally, after about a mile, Mary said, "Megan needed to change clothes. Some kid spilled his Frosty all over her."

"Great," I said. "Megan doesn't need you to change her clothes for her. Besides, if her brother drove her all the way home to New Kassel to change her clothes, why didn't he just drop you off at the house? He had to go right by there. There was no reason for him to bring you all the way back here."

"Mom," she said.

"What?" I asked. "You know, you know you are not supposed to leave the rink with anybody except me or your father or unless I tell you otherwise!"

"But I woulda been there all by myself," she said.

"Mary," I said and skidded to a stop at the light. "There were thirteen—yes, *thirteen*—of your closest friends at that rink tonight. I know because you listed them all off to me as a reason for why you should be there."

She was quiet.

The light had turned green and I hadn't moved fast enough, so the guy behind me laid on his horn. I put the car in park, got out, and walked back to his car. "Excuse me, I realize you're in a hurry," I said to the driver, "but I'm in the middle of a crisis here, and if you could find it in your heart to allow me more than two point four seconds to step on the gas pedal, I'd appreciate it."

The man just gaped at me while I stalked back to my car and gave it gas.

"Oh, my God, Mother," Mary said. "You are seriously PMS-ing."

"PMS-ing? I'll show you PMS-ing."

"Oh, here we go," she said. "I know, I know, I'm grounded from the phone."

"The computer," I said.

"What?" she screeched. Then she pleaded. "No, Mom."

"You wanna talk to me about PMS-ing? You wanna talk to me about how you just scared the ever-loving bejesus out of me?" I said. That wasn't it, though. It wasn't that she scared me. I'd assumed she'd been abducted because I couldn't bear the thought that my little girl would actually go against one of our house rules. A rule Rudy and I had set up for a reason. As a safety precaution. She'd just blithely ignored it. Either she was stupid, which I doubted, or she'd just done the equivalent of giving me a raspberry to my face. That was it. She'd just told me to kiss off, basically. My sweet little girl.

That's what bothered me.

"Fine," she said and shrank down in the seat. I realized then that she hadn't put on her seat belt. Mary will push the limits and try to get by without it, especially in New Kassel, where the speed limit is, like, fifteen miles per hour and she thinks that means she couldn't get hurt in a wreck. Which isn't true at all, of course, but the worst part is that when we're in places like Wisteria that have a higher speed limit she'll forget to put it on.

"Put on your seat belt," I said.

"Why?"

"Because I said so."

"I'd rather leave it off. That way, if we have a wreck, I'll just die and get away from you!"

"Get it on now. It's the law."

"Oh, so you don't care if I die? Is that it? You just want me to wear it because of some stupid law?"

"Mary, I swear, you either get that seat belt on now or I'll shove it up your nose."

"Whatever," she said. But she did put the seat belt on.

When we got home she ran up to her bedroom and slammed the door shut, causing all the pictures in the hallway to move a quarter of an inch to the right.

Rudy found me sitting on the bottom step with my face in my hands. "So, where was she?"

"She'd left the rink with Megan and her older brother," I said.

"What?" he said, anger rising in his eyes.

"Yeah," I said. "I could tell by the look on her face that

she thought she'd gotten back to the rink before I arrived. She knew she wasn't supposed to leave."

"Why'd she do it?"

I shrugged. "Apparently, Megan got something spilled on her clothes, and you know thirteen-year-old-girls can't change their clothes without somebody to hold their hands. But who knows, that could have been an excuse they concocted. That's just it. Now that she's done this, it makes me doubt everything she says."

"I'll talk to her," he said.

"If you talk to her now, it won't do any good. Anything you say will justify everything she's feeling. Wait until tomorrow," I said.

"She's supposed to work the sno-cone stand at the rose show."

"I know," I said, "and she will. I grounded her from the computer."

Rudy smiled because he understood how huge the computer was in Mary's life. Aside from the horses, the computer was everything. "You're good."

"Not good enough," I said, "or I wouldn't have had to do this in the first place."

"Don't blame yourself," he said. "She's being thirteen."

"She's being a brat."

"Brat…thirteen…they're interchangeable."

THE FIRST-EVER ANNUAL New Kassel Rose Show was a success in my book. It was Saturday, and I was doing what I loved best: walking the streets of New Kassel at midday during a festival with the aroma of kettle corn wafting through the trees and the sounds of laughter and Tobias's accordion flitting all around me.

Tobias had insisted that he play his accordion, even though he was in charge of the rose show and had many other things to do. His accordion playing has become somewhat famous regionally. He's been the star of several magazine and newspaper articles, and I think there was a certain amount of pride at stake. He'd rather juggle the rose show and the accordion than have somebody else take over and play for him.

My sister had taken the morning off to have breakfast with her husband and kids at Fraulein Krista's, and now she was taking the afternoon shift at the Gaheimer House, which freed me up to walk the town. I tried not to think about what Mary had done last night. I kept reliving that split second during which I'd thought she'd been abducted, that split second when I wasn't certain where she was or what had happened to her. I could still feel the little prickles of sweat that had beaded on the back of my neck. My God, what must Sandy Kendall have felt when he found Rupert hanging from that tree?

I didn't want to know. If it was one smidgen worse than what I felt last night—and I knew it had to be—I didn't want to know it.

Elmer Kolbe waved at me from across the road, and I waved back. Rachel and Riley were seated on the top rung of Gerri Harold's fence, sharing an ice cream cone. It really disturbed me that the same daughter who would not eat potato chips out of a bag that somebody else had stuck his hand in would now lick an ice cream cone that Riley had licked. I mean, his spit particles were all over that ice cream! I guess it was living proof that Riley was here to stay.

I made my way to the area we had set up for the roses.

They were awarding the blue ribbon for the best fragrance as I walked up. It went to Sam Hill's wife, Janie, for her Golden Celebration. I found the names of roses quite interesting. Walking through the rows of "contestants," I saw names like Betty Boop, Don Juan, Glamis Castle, and Sunsprite. There was also a slew of roses named after famous people like Cary Grant, Queen Elizabeth, Julia Child, and Anne Boleyn. What about Martha Stewart? Is there a rose named after Martha Stewart? There should be. I wonder what you have to do to get a rose named after you.

I stuck my nose in the blue ribbon winner and could not believe the fragrance, light and fruity and like nothing I'd ever smelled before. In fact, it was so wonderful that I just kept right on smelling it. I think I would have stood there with my nose in the rose for the next hour if Sheriff Mort hadn't walked up and spoken to me.

"Show a success?" he asked.

"Yeah," I said. "I think so. Everybody seems pretty happy. Maddie and the gang had an open show where anybody could bring roses in, and they gave away blue ribbons. I didn't know they were going to do that. I thought only the garden club members were going to bring in roses. This turned out to be really neat."

"So we're doing it again next year?" he asked.

"Yeah, I think so," I said.

"Where's Rudy?"

"He took Matthew to the ball game," I said. "Cardinals are playing the Cubs. Can't miss a Cards-Cubs game."

"Well," he said, glancing around, "a lot of people did. You've got quite a crowd here."

"Yes, we do have a great crowd," I said, looking

around at all the people shopping and sniffing roses. "What's up?"

"I got the files on the Kendall suicides," he said.

"And?"

"I looked through them. Where can we talk?"

"How about my office?"

As we walked back toward the Gaheimer House, I saw Eleanore approaching on the sidewalk. It was the third or fourth time I'd seen her since her "incarceration," as she had so eloquently put it, although I hadn't had much chance to speak with her. She wore a hot pink dress that touched the ground, a large hat with at least two dozen freshly cut roses stuck haphazardly in the brim, and an orange ribbon pinned over her heart. Charity Burgermeister told Helen Wickland that ever since her time in jail, Eleanore has worn that orange ribbon over her heart to remind her of the injustice done to her at the hands of Granite County law enforcement. I thought she was going to wave and go on by, but instead she stopped me. "Torie, I would just like to say that the rose show has been an overwhelming success." For the record, she didn't even look at Sheriff Mort.

"Thanks," I said, "but I think the garden club deserves all the credit."

She leaned in with one hand on her hip and said, "And don't you forget it."

"Right," I said.

"Because I'll never forget just how much you did to get me out of jail," she said.

"But Eleanore, I didn't do anything to get you out of jail."

"My point exactly," she said. Then she threw her shoulders back and walked on down the road.

Mort shook his head and smiled. "Who is she, anyway?"

I laughed. "What do you mean?"

"Well, I mean, I know who she is because I had to arrest her, but who is she?"

We walked into the Gaheimer House, and I offered him something to drink, which he declined. Waving to my sister, the sheriff and I ducked into my office quickly, so as not to disturb the tour. He took a moment to look around my office. Pictures of my kids line one end of my desk. Several ceramic items are arranged on the other end. They're mostly things my kids made in art class, and they're ugly as homemade sin, but they were made with heart, which is all that matters. He read some of the titles of books that I had sitting around, mostly histories of the area and compilations of records. Then he came to the antique Rose of Sharon quilt that had hung on my office wall for as long as I could remember. Sylvia had said to me when I first went to work for her, "You get the room with the Rose of Sharon for your office." Funny, I'd never asked her who made it or where it came from. Suddenly, I wondered if she had made it in her youth.

"Nice office," he said.

"Thanks. It's small, but I have a great view of the main street in town right outside my window. It's the office I've had for over ten years. I didn't see any point in moving it once Sylvia died."

"You really care about this town, don't you?"

I smiled. "It's my livelihood—but beyond that, yes, I really do. You know, towns have personalities just like people. I happen to be really compatible with this one."

"Why the move out of town, then?" he asked.

"I don't know." I shrugged. "We were ready for a change of pace, and I think Rudy thought we'd get along better if I wasn't quite in the thick of things so much."

"Has it worked?" he asked. It felt strange having somebody ten years my junior inquire about how my marriage was faring.

"I'm still right in the middle of everything," I said with a laugh. "I think Rudy really just wanted to move to the country and used my involvement with the town as an excuse. I'm not so sure I could have stayed in town, anyway. Not after that whole mess with Bill." Bill, the ex-mayor, had hated me with a passion. He's in jail now, thanks to the fact that I caught him at identity theft. At least he was ahead of the curve. He stole his identity long before it had become the "in" thing to do.

"Well, I'm glad things are going well for you," he said.

"So, what have you got? Are you going to share? The suspense is killing me."

He smiled and his violet eyes shimmered. I'd only seen one other person in the whole world with violet eyes, a girl I'd gone to school with. You couldn't help but be drawn to them. For some reason, they made me trust him a little more than I otherwise would have.

"Well, Rupert's suicide seems totally on the up and up. The investigators interviewed his sister about it. She said that Rupert had been despondent, and she said that when he first came home from the war, he was confused a lot. Half the time he still thought he was in the trenches. Back in France. On the occasions when he realized he was at home, he'd cry and tell Glory that she needed to hide and not let the big man find her. She also talks about him hiding under the bed and even sleeping on the roof. He seemed to be torn between wanting to be in wide-open spaces with lots of air and wanting to be huddled in dark, close quarters. It was as if he felt safe in the trenches but longed to be in the open." Mort shook his head. "War really messes with men."

"I know," I said. "Anything else?"

"Glory also said that in his more lucid moments he understood he was at home and knew who everybody was, but he couldn't get it through his head that the war was over. He thought it was still going on and that he'd have to go back at any moment. No matter how many times Glory would try to tell him that the war was over, he wouldn't believe her."

"So you think he killed himself because he thought he was going to have to go back? He'd rather be dead?" I asked.

Mort shook his head. "According to Glory's testimony, one day Rupert woke up and was normal. Normal for the first time since he'd been back, and he told her that he understood that the war was over. Things were fine for about a week—Glory didn't elaborate on what happened during that week—and then he killed himself. Glory was the one who found him." Mort scratched his head, and I knew there was something he wasn't telling me.

"Does that bother you?" I asked.

"Yeah," he said. "I think Glory may have either assisted him or knew he was going to do it and turned a blind eye to it."

"Why?"

"Because her brother—Whalen—said that he saw her come in from the back porch early in the morning and act as though nothing was wrong, but there was no way she could have been on the back porch and not seen her brother hanging from the tree."

"What could she possibly have done to assist him?" I asked.

He shrugged. "I'm not sure. I'm really just thinking out loud."

"Well, Glory was the one who took care of him and really loved him. She was totally devoted to him. I wonder if she just sat with him while it happened. To comfort him."

"Comfort him?"

"To let him know that she was there and she wouldn't leave him," I said.

"Could be. Seems kinda sick."

"Well, clearly things weren't quite right in that house," I said. "What did Sandy and Whalen have to say?"

"See, this is what makes me suspicious about the whole thing. I mean, I'm sure, based on the physical evidence, that Rupert killed himself. No question about it. But Sandy and Whalen Kendall both say that when Glory came to tell them that Rupert had killed himself, she was totally calm."

"Calm?"

"Yeah, her father even states that he didn't understand why Glory wasn't hysterical. But she wasn't. She calmly said, 'Rupert's gone and hung himself.' Simple as that. So if she didn't actually assist him or sit with him, I think she suspected he was about to do something like that, and I think she found him long before she told anybody. That would have given her time to get her hysterics over with."

"Yeah, and by the time she told her father and brother, the numbness had set in."

"Exactly."

"All right, so what about Glory?" I asked.

"Her suicide is the strangest of all three, and I believe you may be correct, especially if the lab comes back with positive results for strychnine on her sewing things. A neighbor knocked on the Kendall door at about seven the night before her body was discovered. The neighbor thought Whalen seemed really upset, but Whalen claimed he was fine. The neighbor inquired about Glory, and Whalen said she was upstairs sleeping, that she'd taken laudanum to go to sleep."

"Why is that so strange?"

"Because the other neighbor, who loaned them the laudanum, said she didn't loan it to them until almost midnight," Mort said.

I sat down in my chair.

"So…Neighbor A unexpectedly knocks on the door, and Whalen, who's shook up because his sister is already dead, makes up an excuse about the laudanum," I said. "Then later, when he and his father are trying to figure out how to cover this up, they realize they could use the laudanum excuse that Whalen has already laid the groundwork for. Except…"

"They have no laudanum," Mort said.

"Exactly," I said. "So they have to borrow some. Sandy goes to the one person he knows he can blackmail, Neighbor B, the next-door neighbor who is in debt up to her ears, a widow with half-grown children."

"Right. He wouldn't go to the pharmacist, even if the shop was open at that hour, because the records would show what time the laudanum was purchased," Mort said.

"Exactly," I said. "So which one killed her? The father or the brother?"

"I don't know who killed her, but they both covered it up," he said.

"I don't understand," I said. "Why didn't the investigators catch the time discrepancy? They talked to the neighbor who loaned the Kendalls the laudanum. Doris, that's her name."

"Doris Jenkins, to be exact. The answer is, because when they went back to double-check that with her, she changed her story and said that she had been mistaken. She said Whalen had borrowed the laudanum at three in the afternoon the day before."

"The day before?"

"Yes," he said.

"So…Glory could have been dead almost two days before they reported it."

"Sandy and Whalen were shittin' bricks," Mort said. "Excuse the French."

"That's okay. It's appropriate," I said. Then I rubbed my head. "Are you sure you don't want something to drink? I need an infusion."

"If you insist," Mort said.

I grabbed two Dr Peppers and ran back to my office. I handed one to Mort and then sat back down in my chair, popped the can, and started drinking mine.

"So you think one of them killed her?" Mort asked.

"Who else would it have been?"

"A jealous lover?"

I thought of Anthony Tarullo. Could he have been so hurt over being jilted that he snuck into her house and poisoned her sewing pins? "It was personal," I said. "Whoever it was. If my suspicions are correct, they poisoned her quilting pins, for God's sake."

"So you think they were trying to make it look like a suicide?"

"No, think about it. They could have discovered strychnine would not look like a suicide. At least not at first. Once the rigor had passed and without modern toxicology tests, well…then it could pass for a suicide, as it obviously did."

"So whoever it was, even if it was her father or brother, didn't think about covering it up as a suicide until after the fact," Mort said.

"Yeah," I answered, scratching my head, "but…okay, who would have the most to lose if Glory turned up murdered in the house?"

"The father," he said.

"Exactly," I said. "Which means he was the least likely one to do it. So I think it was Whalen."

"Or an outside source," he said. "Because if you had poisoned your sister or daughter with a lethal amount of strychnine, wouldn't you have cleaned up the mess so that nobody else would get poisoned? Or so that you wouldn't accidentally poison yourself?"

"Which brings you to an outside source. Like Anthony Tarullo," I said.

I swallowed the last of my Dr Pepper and explained to Mort who Anthony Tarullo was. "You have to promise me that if it turns out to be Anthony Tarullo we won't say anything about it until his brother passes away. Marty Tarullo is ninety-something and worshipped his brother. It's not like anything can be done about it now, anyway, and I don't want to ruin that for Marty."

"I'm all right with that," Mort said.

"Okay, so what about Whalen's suicide?"

"He went in his brother's room, locked the door, and blew his brains out all over his brother's wall," he said.

"How do you know he locked the door?"

"Because his father said that the door was locked when he heard the gun go off. He got the key and opened the door and there was Whalen."

"Did Sandy give any reason his son would shoot himself?"

"He said that Whalen was completely distraught over both of his siblings dying and his wife and daughter leaving him. That he couldn't go on. Sandy said he'd watched Whalen like a hawk right after Glory died, because he had been afraid that Whalen might do something like this, but he thought the danger had passed."

"That's it?"

"Yeah, except that when the investigators asked why Whalen had gone into his brother's room to do it, instead of his own room, or anywhere else, for that matter, Sandy said that he thought Whalen felt guilty that he had never seen combat and his brother had. Like somehow he'd let his little brother down. Sandy said that Whalen had said on more than one occasion that it wasn't right that Rupert had seen blood spill and he hadn't. That he was the one—as the older brother—who should have been in the trenches, not Rupert. I guess maybe, in his own twisted way, shooting himself in Rupert's room was a way of paying homage to his brother? I honestly don't know."

"So he'd seen the trenches after all," I said. "Just the ones that Rupert had drawn, not the real ones."

"Apparently so," he said.

"Wow."

"Does that answer any of your questions?"

"Sort of. Of course, it raises more questions."

"Most investigations do," he said.

"Well, thank you so much, Sheriff. I really appreciate it."

"No problem," he said. "I'll let you know as soon as the toxicology report comes back on those pins. Oh, by the way, there's something in the kitchen that I brought for you. I had no idea you liked game, but Colin assured me that you did and that you'd really appreciate it. So enjoy, and I'll talk to you later."

Game? What sort of game? I walked Mort to the door and then went back to the kitchen, where I found two big coolers sitting on the countertop. I'd completely passed right over them when I came in to get the two sodas a while ago. My mind had been totally gone. Totally in 1922 with the Kendall family.

I lifted the lid on the first cooler. Inside was a bunch of frozen meat. Game? Oh, no. It was deer meat. Colin knows I don't like deer meat. In fact, I can't even stand to smell the stuff cooking. The second cooler had at least a dozen dead fish in it. I'm not sure it would have been worse if the heads had been cut off, but the little beady eyes stared at me from underneath the ice. I slammed the coolers shut and thought about killing my stepfather. It was bad enough that I had to deal with Rudy's dead fish that he brought in the house, but Mort's, too? A dozen dead fish and deer parts. Just lovely. What did I ever do to deserve such a malicious stepfather?

Okay, don't answer that.

SEVENTEEN

THERE WAS A STRANGE-LOOKING BIRD sitting on my fence. It was late evening after the rose show, and Rudy and I were sitting out on the back patio, listening to the crickets and the katydids. He was wondering about…well, I'm not sure, since his mind is often vacant when he's staring off into space. I was wondering what the heck kind of bird that was. "What sort of bird do you think that is?" I asked.

"Some sort of thrush," he said. "It has spots on its breast."

"How do you know what kind of bird that is?" I asked.

"I had to identify, like, forty species of birds for some summer camp thing I did when I was a kid," he said.

"I did not know that," I said, amazed that after eighteen years together, there were still things I didn't know about him.

"Why did you ask me what kind of bird it was if you didn't think I'd know the answer?" he said.

"I don't know. Just making conversation."

"Women," he said, and laughed. I laughed along with him.

Just then the back door opened. Mary's indignant voice said, "I'm home." Colin had just dropped her off from working the sno-cone stand. She had to stay and clean up afterward. With her tone, she was letting Rudy and me know in no uncertain terms that she was insulted to have to spend the day doing manual labor. She was also making a production of letting us know she was home.

"Great," I said. "Did you have fun?"

"Yeah, right," she said, and shut the door.

Rudy and I exchanged glances, and then he grabbed my hand and squeezed it. "We'll survive her adolescence, don't worry."

"I know," I said. "What worries me is that it's not as if she's doing drugs or having sex. How do we cope if she moves beyond the hormonal, grouchy, smart-mouth, I'm-going-to-test-you-to-the-limit phase?"

"We dig our heels in," he said.

We were quiet a moment. "You think Rachel and Riley are having sex yet?" I asked.

"Oh, Jesus Christ!" he exclaimed. "Don't even go there. Stop. Don't ever say that again!"

I laughed so hard my side hurt.

"Good God, woman. Why would you say something like that?"

"Well, it's not as if she's never gonna—"

"*Don't!*"

"I *hope* she's not having sex yet, but unless we buy her a chastity belt it's going to happen someday. In fact, her future husband probably wouldn't appreciate it if she had a chastity belt."

Rudy glared at me a moment. "You're twisted, you know that?"

As we fell into laughter once more, Mary came back to the door, opened it, and said in the most deadpan casual way possible, "Matthew put something down the toilet. Now it's smoking."

All in all, a typical day in our household.

Rudy went to see what was causing the toilet to smoke

while I went upstairs to my office. I thought about how beautiful the day had been, how perfectly the rose show had unfolded. It would be a nice thing to add to the roster of events in New Kassel. Maybe next year we could have a rose festival. Devote a whole week to roses. We could have experts set up booths and teach people how to grow them, how to prune them, how to keep them from getting diseases, and so forth. It seemed like a brilliant thing to do. I was making a note of that when my phone rang. It was my real estate agent, Sherry Dowdy.

"Hey, Torie, I just wanted to let you know that Mr. Merchant accepted your offer on the Kendall house," she said.

"Great," I said, sitting down. As I often do, I had gone after something and wasn't quite prepared for it when it actually happened. I was going to be the owner of the Kendall house. I would get my museum devoted to women's textile arts. It was real. I was so happy I could have burst. It would be the first really big, important thing I would do in this town that Sylvia had not been involved with in some shape or form. This was all mine. Well, I'd have help, of course, but I'd achieved something outside the Realm of All Things Sylvia.

We talked a bit about when to get together and when to close and all that legal junk.

Rudy walked by my office on his way to the bedroom, and I told him the good news. Then I made a mental note to call Geena Campbell and see if she would help me get this whole thing together. I'd pay her, of course, and I was seriously hoping that she'd agree to stay on one day a week after the initial opening. Oh, my God. My mind was racing with all of the things I would need to do to make this happen.

I called Evan Merchant, and he answered on the third ring.

"Hello, Evan, it's Torie," I said. "Congratulations, you're going to get the money that you need."

"Not a moment too soon," he said. "Congrats to you, too. You're going to get your museum."

"Thanks a bunch," I said.

"I hope you can handle this house," he said.

"Don't worry about me," I said. "Hey, listen, I know it's after eight, but do you think I could come over and look through the house again? The day I was there, I had Geena with me and we were just looking for quilts. Then Rudy went through the house with the real estate agent, so I haven't really gotten to get a good look."

"Not a problem," he said. "I'll have the door unlocked for you."

"Thanks," I said.

"You're not going to change your mind on me, are you?" Evan asked.

"Don't be silly," I said, and hung up the phone. "Rudy, I'm headed over to the Kendall house. I want to do a walk-through."

"Okay," he said. "I'll hold down the fort."

I WAS STEPPING INTO the foyer of the Kendall house within fifteen minutes. Rudy had said the plumbing and electrical systems had been done sometime in the seventies and might need to be replaced in a few years. I flipped the light switch on, and when I did, I swear it sounded like the house moaned. I walked through the big rooms in the front of the house back to the kitchen. There were no modern appliances. An old refrigerator that had the freezer on the bottom and the fridge part on the top was in one corner, and a gas-burning stove that must have been fifty years old sat next to it. The white sink had a dark brown rust or mineral stain in it but otherwise was in good shape. I checked in the cabinets to make sure there were no rodents of unusual size, nor cockroaches of either usual or unusual size. Pest control would have been my first call if there had been.

Instead, my first call was to Sheriff Mort, but not until much later.

After checking over everything on the bottom floor, and realizing that I would have to have the main bathroom completely gutted and rehabbed, just as Rudy had suggested, I made my way upstairs. I wondered about Glory's last trip up these stairs. Was she obliviously heading up to her bedroom, to the poisoned pins and her death? All right, I didn't know for sure that the pins were poisoned, but Maddie Fulton lying in the Wisteria General hospital bed went a long way to convince me. I was just waiting on the toxicology report to confirm my suspicions, not arouse new ones.

I pushed open the door to Rupert's room. The hinges creaked. I stood there in the dark for about twenty seconds, just listening to the house. Houses make noise. Houses breathe and settle and morph the exterior sounds into the interior ones. Hey, if Mort can have fish talk to him, I can have a house do the same. The feeling I got from this house was *Tread lightly*. Not *Get out and don't come back,* like Amityville, and not *Come in and stay forever,* like the Walton home. No, it was just *Tread lightly*. I flipped on the light switch and was once again assaulted by Rupert's mural. This time, I studied each wall carefully.

The detail in the drawings was astounding. He captured fear and dread like Rockwell had captured wholesomeness and all-American. There was also whimsy here and there. Like, one part showed five men sitting around playing poker. One of the men had a bullet through his head and was obviously dead, but the funny part was that the player next to him had an ace up his sleeve. They all went on with their game as though the guy next to them hadn't been killed while they played. It made me wonder if that had really happened to Rupert at some point in the trenches.

Another comical scene showed a soldier asking for forgiveness from the priest, and he had his fingers crossed behind his back. All of these images, the horrible and the whimsical, ran together and spread along the walls of Rupert's bedroom like some giant and ancient graphic novel.

If you started as soon as you entered the room on the left and came all the way around, the bloodstains from Whalen's suicide were all over the third wall or third panel in the mural. The bloodstains were about four and a half feet up the wall with heavy splatters on the bottom. Just to the right of his blood was a drawing of Glory Anne, sitting in a chair and quilting, a smile on her face and her hair falling loosely around her shoulders. Rupert's ideal was to leave the trenches and come home. But hovering behind Glory Anne was a twisted and broken figure with his gnarly fingers about to snatch her up and do horrible things to her. The evil man was huge and hulking, but there was no way that I could identify the face, because Rupert had drawn it to look nonhuman. In fact, he looked a bit like Nosferatu, though I'm not sure that had been Rupert's intent. I have no idea when that old silent movie even came out.

I studied the bloodstains and understood why nobody had ever tried to cover them up. If they had, they would have covered up Rupert's masterpiece. I think Evan would have probably painted over the whole room if given half a chance, but he hadn't been able to stay in the house. The owner before him clearly had realized the historical and artistic value of this trench mural and had left it. I was going to call a history professor in St. Louis to come and study this and have it photographed professionally. I wanted to leave this room exactly as it was. I would give tours of it. I supposed I would have to put an age restriction on the tours, not just because of the bloodstains but also because of the subject matter and disturbing images. I decided right then and there that nobody under eighteen would see this, unless their parents saw it first and then allowed them to go in.

Who was the monster that Rupert had drawn on the point of devouring his sister? Who did he represent? Anthony Tarullo? Whalen? Did he represent mankind in general? Or was it just an embodiment of a nightmare that Rupert had had to endure? I could never know for sure.

I suddenly realized that it was exceptionally quiet outside. When I checked my cell phone, it said the time was half past ten. I'd been here almost two hours. It didn't seem like it.

I stood there another half hour examining the bloodstains. Had Whalen chosen this particular part of the wall to shoot himself on purpose? Was there a method to his madness? On the other side of the blood was an image of the sun setting on a soldier's corpse. Something wasn't right. Or maybe it wasn't that there was something wrong, but there was something…something that I just wasn't seeing.

I walked the halls and found an empty bedroom. I guessed that this had been Whalen's room and that the previous owner had cleared it out to sleep in. I peeked in Glory's room, but quite frankly, I was a bit afraid to touch anything in there. I thought the poison had been confined to her pins, but I wasn't taking any chances. I walked back down to what had been Sandy Kendall's room. The bed was exceptionally big. I've seen a lot of antique furniture—you can't live in a town like New Kassel and not have seen a ton and a half of antiques—but I'd never seen a bed this large. I didn't remember any reports saying Sandy had been obese, but I did remember the article mentioning that he was taller than average height, and so was Glory. Based on that sculpture at her grave and things I had read, Glory was probably about five foot ten. That's not unusual by today's standards, but back then, she would have been very tall. My great-grandmother, my Grandma Gert's mother, was six feet tall, and in every picture I have of her with other people, she is towering over them.

That made me think.

In what I assumed had been Sandy's room, I began rifling through drawers and trunks until I found an old photo album in the chest. Next to his father's Civil War uniforms and diaries, a worn and faded velvet-covered photo album lay waiting for someone to discover it. I opened it and began looking at the pictures. From the photo they'd printed of him in the paper when Whalen had killed himself, and a picture in the album that had his name penciled in on the back, I had no trouble recognizing Sandy. I finally found what I was looking for. A family photo.

It wasn't anything formal. It showed Sandy, his wife, Whalen, Rupert, and Glory. It had to have been taken right before Sandy's wife died, because Glory looked as though she could have passed for sixteen or seventeen, and the boys were obviously grown. They were standing out in front of the house. Sandy towered over Whalen and Rupert, but Glory, even as a very young adult, was already nearly as tall as Whalen.

I sifted through more pictures until I found a photograph of Sandy and his two sons, taken after Rupert had come back from the war. I could tell this by several clues. One was that Rupert looked as though he was wearing army boots and had the army haircut. Rupert also had that vacant shell-shocked look on his face, the look he only seemed to have after he went to France. That meant the photograph had been taken when Whalen and Rupert were grown men.

Sandy still towered over them. Head and shoulders over them. Had he been so tall that his bed had been specially made? Why did his height matter?

Well, it's one of those things that happens with my brain. It grabs hold of some tiny thread without realizing that the thread is leading to a bigger string, which will lead to a massive rope. Sandy's height mattered because it made me think of Whalen's height, and Whalen's height mattered because...

The bloodstains. I walked back to Rupert's room, realizing that unless Whalen was extremely short, the stains were in the wrong place. I sat down on the floor with my back to the wall and then turned my head over my shoulder and looked. I'm not tall by any means, but even if Whalen had been six to eight inches taller than I was, the stains would be too high. If I stood up, they were too low. If he kneeled? Maybe. But why would he kneel?

I flipped open the cell phone and called Sheriff Mort. "I know this is going to sound strange," I said, "but could you meet me at the Kendall house with a crime scene investigator?"

"It's eleven. Going on midnight," he said.

"I know," I said. "I suppose it could wait for tomorrow, but—"

"It can wait until tomorrow," he said.

"You don't even know what I want," I said.

"Whatever it is has gone this long without being investigated. It can wait until tomorrow."

"Okay, what time tomorrow?" I said.

"I'll be there at eight," he said. "Bring doughnuts."

"I will," I said.

"What are we looking for?" he asked.

"Bloodstains. Blood splatter."

"The stain on the wall I saw that one time I was there looking for squatters?"

"Yeah," I said.

"What's the angle on this?"

"That's just it. I need to know the angle."

"All right," he said. "Hey, how'd you like the game I left for you?"

"It was…wonderful," I said with no strain in my voice whatsoever.

"Good. I got three deer this past year. I was afraid it was

all going to get freezer burnt and go to waste. Glad you could help me out."

"I...You're welcome. See you tomorrow."

I locked up the house and went home.

EIGHTEEN

THE REALLY HORRIBLE THING about being me is that I'm so obsessive over things that I make myself miserable. All I'd have to do is say to myself, "Self, quit being so obsessive. Go to bed. You don't need to know how tall Whalen Kendall was tonight. You can find that out tomorrow." But Self won't let me do that. Self says, "You have to know, you have to know, you have to know." So then I tiptoe out of my bedroom at one in the morning and quietly enter my office and find the file I made on the Kendalls and look up how tall Whalen was based on his World War I draft papers. He was five foot eight.

He was even shorter than Rupert, but still of average height for men a hundred years ago. I found it strange that Rupert and Whalen had not inherited their father's extreme height. Based on photographs, Sandy must have been six foot six or more. I wondered if maybe Sandy had a disease or genetic disorder that made him exceptionally tall. Like, what was that thing that Abraham Lincoln had? He had a disease that made him extra tall and made his limbs grow long and lanky. Maybe it was something like that.

At any rate, I now knew how tall Whalen was, which would help the CSI and the labs determine the trajectory of that bullet.

I was wide-awake now, so I logged on to the Internet to

do some surfing. I noticed that Mary's little icon thingie was showing up on my buddy list. Mary was on the computer. Mary, who was grounded from the computer. Mary was on the computer, when she was grounded, at one in the morning. Granted, it wasn't a school night, but last I saw her she was snoring her little head off.

She was definitely pushing my buttons.

I went to her room and could see the glow from the computer screen spilling out into the hallway. I stood at the door and watched her typing away and giggling over something that one of her buddies had just sent her. Her back was to me, and I wondered how close I could get to her and the computer without her knowing. I decided that I couldn't get close enough, but I still wanted to know what she was saying. So I ran down to the kitchen and got the binoculars that I keep in the window. Out in the country I find that I need binoculars a lot. Way more than I ever thought I would.

I ran back up the steps, repositioned myself at her bedroom door, and raised the binoculars. Now I could read what she was typing and what was being said back to her. Here's the way her conversation went:

Mary:	He sooooo does like you.
Megan:	No way. He likes Lexy.
Mary:	She's such a loser.
Megan:	At least she's not as bad as Nikki Bittermeyer. I heard she stuck her tongue down some guy's throat.
Mary:	No! Gross!

Thank God, she still thought tongues in other people's throats were gross.

Megan: Can't believe you got grounded.

Mary: My mom is so uncool.

Me? I am not uncool!

Megan: No, your mom is cool. She's just way
                overprotective.

Mary: She's a weirdo.

I am not a weirdo. I couldn't believe that Megan was
sticking up for me and my own daughter was being such
a little twit.

Megan: I never said she wasn't a weirdo. But
                at least she cares.

Mary: Guess you're right. But I hate her
                anyway.

Megan: Why?

Mary: Because I can! I'm an American!
                Besides, she's always right. I hate
                that.

Megan: You're a brat. ☺

Mary: Like you should talk.

Megan: Well, I heard that Tony for sure does
                like you.

Mary: I am not sticking my tongue down
                his throat.

I really wanted to march right over there and jerk a knot
in her tail, but then I'd just give fuel to her fire. The fire
that had my name all over it. Yes, she was grounded, and
she was technically in the wrong, but if I went over there

now and yanked her off of the computer, somehow I'd be the bad guy. Instead I went back to my office and waited until she logged off and went to sleep. Then I sent her an e-mail. It said:

> Mary, when you're ungrounded from the computer you'll get to read this. I just wanted to let you know that I think you're a really cool kid. And I love you very much. I hope when you become a mother you'll understand how hard all of this is. I think we'll go ahead and dye your hair black, since you really want to do that. I want you to be you. I just want you to be safe being you. That's all.
>
> Love, Mom
>
> P.S. I'm changing the passwords on your computer tomorrow night, just in case you're tempted to get online.

With that, I logged off and went to bed and slept soundly until my alarm went off at six thirty.

I STOPPED BY Pierre's bakery in town and picked up some doughnuts, croissants, muffins, and Danishes. When I got to the Kendall house, Sheriff Mort was already there waiting for me. A storm had moved in overnight and left all the grass and leaves wet and the ground dark with moisture. The morning glory was blooming its head off, and Mort stood by it, apparently studying it. "This is a morning glory," he said.

"Yup."

"I saw this in bloom the other evening when I checked the house for you."

"Yup."

"That's not possible," he said.

"Nope," I said and held up the bag of goodies.

"Oh, doughnuts," he said. "I brought the java."

I don't drink coffee, so I begged off and drank my bottled water with my cherry-cheese Danish. The CSI was not there yet, so Mort and I sat down on the front porch and prepared to wait.

"Whalen Kendall was five foot eight," I said. "For the record."

"Okay," he said.

"I want you to see if the trajectory lines up. I want you to check it as if he was sitting, kneeling, and standing when he shot himself."

"Well, obviously you've already got an idea that it's not gonna match up or you wouldn't have hauled me out here on a Sunday morning."

I like Mort. Young, smart, and intuitive. He knows more about the way I think than Colin does, and I've only known Mort for about six months. We'd only worked one real case together, and yet he understood that if I didn't question something, I wouldn't bother him.

The CSI finally showed up. I recognized her from a few other cases I'd been involved in, although I'd never actually been introduced. "Hi," she said. "I'm Darla."

"Nice to meet you," I said.

"Oooh, doughnuts," she said, and began chomping one. Darla was short, dark, and exceptionally congenial.

When she finished eating, we made our way through the house and up the stairs to Rupert's room. "Here's the blood," I said. "I don't want the sketches around it to be disturbed, though, if at all possible."

Darla looked carefully at the wall and then said, "That shouldn't be a problem."

I went out onto the front porch and made some business calls while Darla did her thing. I called Professor Nathaniel Whitaker, a historian, teacher, and biographer who lives in St. Louis and teaches at Oldham University. We've collaborated on some research projects, and he considers the history of New Kassel one of his "hobbies." He picks certain areas—a city, a community within a city—and certain eras, like Victorian or colonial, and then learns everything he can about them. Since his area of expertise is the First World War and the first quarter of the century, his interest was piqued when I started the conversation with "I've discovered an amazing piece of World War I history." He agreed to come out and study the mural and bring a photographer.

Geena Campbell called to tell me that she had a woman interested in depositing three of her grandmother's quilts with us in the museum, whenever we got it up and running. I hadn't even closed on the Kendall house yet, and I had items lined up to go in the museum. I found this very exciting.

Right before lunch, Mort came out onto the porch and motioned me back up to Rupert's room. "I think you need to call an art historian, too," he said.

"Oh, that's a good idea," I said. "I never thought of that."

"And maybe a restorer or somebody who can tell you what's been done to this part right here," he said. I watched him point at the corner where the sketch of Glory Anne was.

"What?" I said.

"That," he said, and stepped closer. He pointed to the

monster, the Nosferatu look-alike, that hovered behind Glory Anne. "That's been messed with. That's not the original drawing."

Goose bumps danced along my spine. "What do you mean, that's not the original? How do you know?"

"I studied art before I became a sheriff," he said. "Can't make a living at it. I can make a living carrying a gun, not a paintbrush. Anyway, that's been messed with. I can tell. See, that's two different pencil leads."

I dialed my cell phone without even looking. There was only one person I knew personally who would know an art historian off the top of his head. "Professor Whitaker, please." When I got off the phone, the historian, the photographer, and the art historian/restorer were all set up to come and see Rupert's mural the next day.

I sighed and watched Darla frame the room in what seemed like a hundred different red laser lights. "I'll be back," I said.

I went to the Gaheimer House to catch up on some work. I needed to keep busy so as to not think about Darla and Mort back at the Kendall house. My dad surprised me by stopping by my office to see if I wanted to get some lunch. We went to Fraulein Krista's to eat, and he told me all about his new hollow-body guitar. Of course, things digressed to politics after that. I don't do well in political talks. I get too angry because I feel helpless to change anything. Dad loves political talks because he gets to call a bunch of people a lot of really bad names with no repercussions. It makes him feel better. Three hours later, I asked for the check. I think Krista was glad to see us go, but I was fairly grateful that my dad had taken me to lunch.

Not only did it make the time go by faster, but I hadn't seen him in what seemed like a month of Sundays. I missed him. Funny how even as a grown-up, I can still miss my mom and dad. Of course, I see my mother every week, so I don't get as much of a chance to miss her.

I did some shopping. I stopped in Norah's Antiques, which is actually owned by Colin. He only works one day a week in the shop. The rest of the time he's doing mayor types of things. Today he was behind the counter. "Hey," he said. He was reading *Fish & Wildlife* with his feet up on the counter and his stool leaned all the way back to the wall. "What's up?"

"I wanted to see if you had any old milk cans. I want to set one out in the yard for decoration."

"I probably do," he said. "What's going on with the Kendall thing?" He came from behind the counter and wandered into a very disorganized and cluttered corner of the store. When Norah owned the shop, it was very neat, orderly, and feminine. She'd carried quite a lot of items that made it look chic and maybe even a little Victorian. Colin bought it, and within a few months it looked like an indoor flea market, with lots and lots of antique fishing gear. He moved an old wooden Coca-Cola carton, and beneath it was a milk can that had been used on dairy farms.

"Cool," I said, ignoring his question. "How much?"

"Fifteen," he said.

I had no idea if that was a good price or not. The only way I can tell with antiques is by finding the same item at five different stores and comparing prices. If they're all relatively the same, then I know that the item is most likely worth that. I trust Colin, though, and he might have even given me the wholesale cost on it. We might fight like cats and dogs, but I do trust him to do what's right. "I'll take it," I said.

"So, what's going on with the Kendall thing?" he asked again.

"Mort is over at the house right now with a CSI doing a trajectory analysis on that blood splatter," I said.

You would have thought I said that a dozen naked Playboy bunnies were jumping rope outside. He got a faraway look in his eyes, and I could see the yearning in his expression. "Blood splatter analysis, huh?"

"Yeah."

"Which CSI?"

"Darla," I said.

"Oh, she's the best," he said.

"Good."

"So…what made you decide to have the stains tested?"

"I don't think Whalen shot himself."

"No?" he asked.

"No. Trajectory is all wrong." I handed Colin the money for the milk can. "I gotta get back over there. They should be about finished. I hope."

"Can I go with you?" he blurted.

"No," I said. "You've got the shop."

"It's Sunday. I close in an hour anyway," he said.

"Well, all right," I said. "Just meet me over there."

"What do you think happened to Whalen?" he asked.

"I think somebody else shot him."

NINETEEN

TURNS OUT, COLIN MADE the trip to the Kendall house and closed the shop early for nothing. Darla had no immediate answer for me. Nobody had immediate answers for me, so I had to go home on that Sunday evening and watch TV. It was the only thing I could do to take my mind off the fact that some stupid lab somewhere held all the answers that I needed. I ended up watching *Shrek* with my son. We shoved our faces full of popcorn, followed up with some Fig Newtons. I eat when I'm nervous. Okay, I just eat, but that's beside the point. Turns out Matthew wants to be an ogre when he gets older, because ogres can smell and nobody cares. I love children's logic. It's so pure. He fell asleep on my lap, and Rudy carried him to bed, complaining that either Matthew was way too big for his age or his back was getting old.

At about two, I managed to force myself to go to sleep, and I awoke the next morning feeling like a kid who's about to go to Disney World—exhausted but overwhelmingly excited. I had three experts coming to look at Rupert's mural today. In the middle of the night, my ordinary eyelids had been replaced with little pieces of sandpaper, and my brain had skipped about three seconds ahead of the rest of my body. I'd think about reaching for the orange juice, but then it wouldn't happen for, like, three seconds.

Mary said nothing to me about the e-mail I'd sent her, so I assumed she hadn't gotten the chance to sneak her mail before I changed the password. She ate her cereal with her hair hanging half in her face, narrowly missing the milk in the bowl. Rachel twittered about, merrily making Eggo waffles and drowning them in a gallon of syrup. It was the last week of school for the year. No wonder she was so happy. Mary was still pouting about getting grounded, or she would have been just as happy. Although Mary wasn't human until almost noon, so maybe she wasn't pouting. I finally got everybody off to school and then dropped Matthew off at my mom's so I could meet Professor Whitaker at the Kendall house.

Professor Whitaker is much like the archetype of what I've always thought a history professor is supposed to be: older, with white hair, a crooked tie, ink stains on his fingers, and lots of nose hairs. Okay, maybe that's not everybody's idea of what a history professor looks like, but it's mine, and Nathaniel Whitaker fits it perfectly. He speaks with a slight eastern accent, like maybe he spent his formative years in Boston, and he smells like chalk dust and brown sugar.

He introduced me to his two colleagues. Roy Hrabowski was the photographer, and Emilia Leon was the art historian/restorer. Roy was one of those ordinary types that I would forget as soon as he left here today, while Emilia could not have been more exotic if she tried. She had dark, dark black hair and pale white skin. Dark eyes peered behind bright blue cat-eye glasses. If I didn't know any better I'd swear those were the exact glasses that my cousin had worn in her third-grade year back in 1966. Emilia wore a red blouse and a long black skirt with a very large and brilliant silver belt and buckle.

"This is amazing," Emilia said as she peered around the room.

"I know," I said. "World War I is not my area of expertise, but I have read about how horrible the trench warfare was. I think Rupert captured it perfectly."

"Historically, artistically, it's brilliant," Professor Whitaker said.

"From a human standpoint as well," Emilia added. "What do you plan to do with it?"

"I plan on opening a textile and quilt museum here," I said. "Rupert's sister was an incredible quilter, nationally recognized. She won an award in San Francisco at the World's Fair. So I don't plan to change a thing in this room. It'll be part of the museum."

Emilia's gaze went to the back of the door. "Are those claw marks?"

"Yes," I said. "I'm not sure when they were made, but I know that Rupert was uncontrollable at times."

I wanted Emilia to get a chance to study the whole mural, but I made a special point of showing her the part that I really wanted her opinion on: the monsterlike creature trying to claim Rupert's sister.

As the trio got to work, my cell phone rang. It was Mort. Maybe he was calling with trajectory news. "Hello?"

"Hi," he said. "The pins came back with traces of strychnine. Probably the only thing that saved Maddie was the fact that there was so little of the poison left on the pins."

"Then Glory was murdered for sure."

"Yes," he said. "Looks that way. Unless she committed the most bizarre suicide in history. But I can't believe with all the ways to kill herself, she'd pick something as painful as strychnine and then go to all the trouble to put it on her sewing pins, rather than just ingesting it outright. It especially makes no sense when you realize she could have gotten her hands on laudanum, for real, if she'd wanted to."

I was silent.

"Are you there?"

"Yeah," I said. The poor girl had been murdered. In her own house. By some despicable person who used her quilting—the one thing she loved—against her. I had expected this. Hell, I was the one who thought from the get-go she had been murdered. Even so, hearing Mort tell me I was right was a little weird—as if at the last minute I was hoping I had been wrong. "That's really crappy."

"I thought so, too. How's it going there?" he asked.

"Oh, we just got started."

"I'll let you know if I hear anything else."

"Thanks," I said.

I hung up the phone and wondered about Glory Anne Kendall. Who would have wanted to kill her? Her father was crazy about her. He went to all the trouble to get special dispensation to have her buried next to him and his wife. I was right on that. He knew she hadn't committed suicide, so I would bet money that he confessed this knowledge, and the priest allowed her to be buried in the Catholic cemetery.

Was Whalen capable of murdering his sister? He was obviously a controlling individual, but did that mean he could have killed her? And not just killed her in a rage, but meticulously planned her murder ahead of time? Why would he have done such a thing? Had Glory decided to marry Anthony Tarullo anyway, and that news sent Whalen off the deep end? Even then, what sort of brother kills his sister over a bad love match? Wouldn't he have taken his anger out on Tarullo instead? Or even killed Tarullo? Who did that leave? Anthony Tarullo?

If it was Anthony Tarullo, why would Sandy and Whalen go to all the trouble of covering his back? Why not say Glory was murdered, have an investigation opened, and get the news out to the public? I would want my sister's or daughter's murderer brought to justice. Why cover it up for him? The very act of making the murder look like a suicide suggested guilt on the parts of both the brother and the father.

My cell phone rang again and I jumped. I didn't recognize the number. "Hello?"

"Torie O'Shea?" a female voice asked.

"Yes," I said.

"Hi, it's Judy Pipkin," she said.

"Oh, hi," I said.

"Marty said you might want to speak to me."

"Marty…Tarullo? Why would he tell you that?" Although it was true, I still wanted to know why Mr. Tarullo would think to share this with Judy Pipkin. As far as I could remember, I never mentioned her name to him when I spoke to him about Glory.

"Because I'm Doris Jenkins's granddaughter," she said. "My mother was ten years old when Glory Kendall died. My mom's older sister, Tilda, married Marty. I think I might have some information for you."

I'VE KNOWN JUDY PIPKIN my whole life. I went to high school with her youngest son, David. Judy is about sixty-eight and worked on the county cemetery project with me, as well as a few other projects involving the historical society. That's a great thing about the people of New Kassel. They may not hold an office or even belong to the historical society, but from time to time they will jump in and help on a project, either because that particular project is near and dear to them for whatever reason, or because they just have the spare time and decide to help out. At any rate, Judy Pipkin really enjoyed historical work, though not the touristy stuff so much. She lives in the house right next to the Murdoch Inn. Sandwiched in between the Murdoch and the Old Mill Stream restaurant, right where the road bends, it's a beautiful Colonial home that was built in the forties.

I knocked on her door a half-hour later, and she answered right away. "Hi, Judy," I said.

"Torie, come in," she said, waving me indoors. "How's your mother?"

"Oh, she's doing great. She's got her hands full with Colin right now," I said.

"I've heard that he's going stir-crazy," she said. "One rumor even said that he was thinking about resigning as mayor and going back to being sheriff."

"He can't do that," I said. "Mort is in office." I said that more for my comfort than to quell any rumors she may have been spreading. Judy is a thin and wiry woman, with lots of dark hair for her age. I know she doesn't color it, because she has plenty of gray around the temples. That's where the gray stops, though. It doesn't spread around her head like mine. Now that I thought about it, I realized she had less gray than I did, and I'm almost thirty years her junior. I couldn't help but wonder why Mother Nature was so inconsistent.

"Listen," she said, "I heard you were looking into the Kendall suicides."

"Yes," I said. "I bought the Kendall house."

"Oh, that's great," she said. "I'm so glad somebody is looking into this. Somebody who can tell the story right."

"Well, I don't know if I can do that or not, but I'll try."

"My mother always told me that she thought the girl, Glory, had been murdered."

"Based on the whole laudanum thing?"

"Yes," she said.

"Did she have any ideas as to suspects?" I asked.

"Mom said that Glory was one of those girls who just got too much attention."

"What do you mean?"

"Her brother-in-law didn't just love Glory, he worshipped her. According to my mom, he would have killed for Glory," she said.

"Your mom would have been pretty young at the time. Are you sure about this?"

"I'm only telling you what she told me her whole life. Whether or not she witnessed this stuff, or if maybe her mother told her, I don't know, but my mother was adamant. Anthony would have done anything for Glory Kendall."

"People throw phrases like that around pretty loosely. Sitting at the drive-up window at the bank the other day I was saying how I was going to kill the teller if she didn't hurry up. Are you sure she meant it literally?"

Judy shrugged. "Of course, I can't know for sure, but I

think she was serious. Anyway, she said that everybody felt very strongly about Glory. You couldn't just like her or tolerate her, you adored her or worshipped her. Everybody felt that way about her, and I mean everybody." She narrowed her eyes and cut them around her living room.

"What are you saying?"

"I'm saying her brothers were no different than anybody else."

It was really quiet in her living room.

"Are you saying that…her brothers…*loved* her? Were in love with her? Like in the biblical sense?" I asked, hysteria rising in my voice. It couldn't be true. It made sense, it would make everything make sense, but it just couldn't be true.

"I'm saying that my mother said that her brothers—I can't remember their names—fought for her attention. The older one couldn't stand it that the younger one got the attention because he had been to war, so he'd try to get his sister's attention in other ways."

Hazel left Whalen right after Sophie was born. Was that why? Because she sensed or maybe even discovered that Whalen was in love with his sister? It would sure as hell be enough reason for me to leave, if I'd been in her shoes, and like her, I would have taken my daughter and most likely would have tried to keep her from him. They didn't have "joint custody" back then. If Whalen had wanted Sophie, he would have gotten her. How horrible to find out your husband was in love with another woman, especially when the other woman was his sister!

Could this be the Big Thing? The big secret that all of this was wrapped up in?

It hadn't even occurred to me—most likely because, at

the core of it all, I still expect the best from people, not the worst. I'm not sure if that makes me pathetically naive or the last of a dying breed. Maybe both.

"Listen, Judy, do you remember ever hearing anything about Whalen's wife? Whalen was the older brother. His wife, Hazel, left him. Does any of this ring a bell with you?"

"You know, I don't remember names," she said, and it's all pretty vague. I just remember the things my mother was the most adamant about. I do recall her mentioning that one of the boys had a wife and that she'd disappeared. That's all I remember about it, though. Marty would be the one you should ask."

Of course! When I talked to Marty, I'd been so wrapped up in the Glory/Anthony love story that I'd completely forgotten to mention Hazel. I guess at the time I hadn't seen how that would actually have affected Glory. If what Judy said was right, it could shed some light on why Hazel had left. Of course, like so much family history, this was just one woman's secondhand knowledge.

Judy's phone rang then. She went into the kitchen to answer it, was gone a few moments, and then came back into the living room. "It's Marty Tarullo's daughter," she said. "He's had a stroke. He's asking to speak to you."

"To me?" I asked, shocked.

"He's at Wisteria General," she said. "I'll drive you."

TWENTY

MARTY TARULLO HAD SLIPPED in and out of consciousness for the five hours that I was at Wisteria General. I made a phone call to Professor Whitaker, and he said that the team would be back the next day, too. Emilia was hard at work on restoring the original drawing of the monster character in the mural. How she was doing this I didn't know, and I didn't care. I just wanted to see what was beneath the current drawing. Finally, I'd had Rudy come pick me up and take me to my car at Judy's house. I'd asked the hospital to call me when Marty came to. I had no idea what he wanted to tell me, but in case it was something that could blow this whole Kendall family mystery wide open, I sure as heck wasn't going to sit on my hands. If he wanted to talk to me, by golly, I'd be there. I followed Rudy home with my mind feeling like it was expanding, pushing out of my ears and eye sockets until I thought my head would explode. I know that expanding your mind is supposed to be a good thing, but I would have argued that point right then.

When I got home, I made a list of things to do to prepare for the Strawberry Festival coming up in June. Then I vacuumed all the floors. I vacuumed the living room floor three times. Not because it needed it, but just because I forgot that I'd already done it and did it again. Finally, when I was about ready to start the vacuum for the fourth time, Rudy threatened to make me go live in the stables. That would have been bad, so I put away the vacuum.

I decided to walk out to the stables and see the horses that Rudy had threatened me with. I hadn't given them very much attention since this whole Kendall thing had started. I wanted to spend an evening just doing nothing and not thinking about the Kendalls. It was scary how I could immerse myself in somebody else's family so completely that I started to feel betrayed when they didn't behave like I thought they should, hurt when tragedy ultimately struck, and stumped when I didn't understand their motivation.

I love to hear horses breathe. That may sound strange, but nobody ever said that I was normal. In fact, my own mother has never said it, and my daughters routinely call me "weird" or "unusual." I walked through the stable, listening to the horses breathe and the crickets rub their legs together and the owl in the distance ask, "Who?"

When the temperature felt as though it had dropped below sixty, I headed back into the house. I took a book off the shelf in the living room and started to read. I fell asleep there and was awakened by Rudy kissing my forehead the next morning.

Wow, horses must be magic. I slept really soundly and had not thought of the Kendalls at all. Not until this very moment when I woke up. I'm pretty predictable, huh?

Rudy took Matthew to my mother's, and I saw to it that Mary didn't go to school with black lipstick on. Then I headed up to my bathroom. Just as I stepped out of the shower, my phone rang.

It was Judy Pipkin. "Torie, he's awake. If you want to see him, you should probably get here fast. I can't say how long he's going to be lucid, and I don't think he'll last through the day."

"I'll be right there," I said.

I HATE VISITING the terminally ill, and without a miracle, Marty Tarullo was not long for this world. I want people to be either alive or dead. That whole hanging on in a world that no longer has a place for you…it's just horrible. I suppose one good thing could come of it, if you're inclined to take advantage of it. It could give you a chance to say things to the people you need to say things to, before diving off into the wild blue yonder.

Marty Tarullo was doing just that. Not only had he requested to speak to me, but he was surrounded by his family. He'd been saying the things he needed to say. I have respect for that. His family will cherish his last words in the years to come. His hospital room was not cheery in the least. Nobody'd had the chance to bring in colorful balloons with cutesy sayings on them or vases full of fragrant flowers. But his family was here, and that was the most important thing.

When I walked in, I felt like I was interrupting. Well, I was. These were his last moments with his family, yet he'd chosen to give a few of these moments to me. His family had to give up precious time that they would never get back to allow him to talk to a relative stranger. Connie recognized me when I entered the room. She smiled and said to her father, "Dad, Torie O'Shea is here."

His eyes wandered around a bit until his gaze landed firmly on me. I gave a slight wave and walked over to his bedside. There must have been seven or eight people in the room. They all smiled at me and nodded.

The milky white lights did nothing to make Marty look any less close to death than he was. In fact, they made him look as though he'd already passed on. If it had been my father lying there, I'd have opened the window. My father loves the sun on his face and the smell of the outdoors, and I couldn't take him looking like this. Maybe it had been too distracting for Marty.

"Hi, Mr. Tarullo," I said in a quiet voice. It still sounded loud.

"Missus O'Shea," he said, and grabbed my hand. His hand was soft and cool. His voice came out almost a whisper. "I wanted to ask a favor of you."

I glanced around the room, uncertain what he was about to ask. "If I can do it, I will."

"Would you…" He took a deep breath. "Would you continue putting flowers on Glory Anne's grave for me? Once I'm gone, everyone will forget."

A sniffle came from somewhere in the room, and I have to admit, a lump bulged in the back of my throat. I barely knew the man, but his devotion was utterly heartbreaking. Even on his deathbed, he could not forget the woman who was Glory Anne Kendall. Really, he couldn't forget his brother, either, because this tradition of putting flowers on Glory's grave was for his brother.

"Of course," I said.

"Every June," he instructed.

"Every June," I repeated.

His grip loosened and his hand fell limply to his chest. Instinctively I checked to see if he was still breathing, and he was. No monitors went off, and his chest rose every few seconds. The brief exchange with me had worn him out. I looked to his daughter, who was dabbing her eyes. "I don't understand," I said. "He could have just asked any one of you to ask me for this favor. Why did he want me here?"

"Because he wanted to see your face when you answered. He wanted to know whether or not you were sincere," she said. "He hated telephones for that reason. He said you couldn't really tell what people were thinking unless they were right in front of you."

It made sense to me, and I was deeply honored that he chose me to carry on this tradition. "What are the doctors saying?" I asked.

"His heart is giving out," she said. "He'll go into a coma before long, and he'll just slip away."

I said my apologies to her and decided that I'd intruded enough. I backed out of the door silently and headed for Fraulein Krista's for a hot fudge sundae.

Okay, so I eat when I'm sad. So what? I've been doing it for almost forty years and it's never failed to make me feel…less hungry. At the end of the sundae, I was still sad, but the sundae had been good, and that was something. Right?

Sitting there at the table in my favorite restaurant in town, steeped in Bavarian polka music and the smells of sauerkraut and bratwurst, I came to a startling conclusion. I hate loose ends. I hate ambiguity. I hate random acts. I hate misrepresentation. I hate it when people such as the Kendalls had shown themselves one way to the public, when they were something else entirely in private. I mean, I know all families have their "public faces" and their "private faces," but the Kendalls lived double lives. When does that start to become a problem? When does that double life start to eat away at a person and cause him or her to start breaking down?

I have a cousin who has a lot of the same childhood memories that I have because we spent a ton of time together. When you hear her recall these memories, and then you hear me tell the same stories, they are very different. I remember my grandparents' farm as a lot of fun, but not all fun. Every magical stroll through the berry patch that I took, I got chased by bumblebees half the time. Although the baby chickens were cute, I sat in chicken poop more often than not. Yes, Grandma taught me about making strawberry jam, and Grandpa would sit on the porch and play the violin, but a great deal of the time I sat around wishing to God they got more than three black-and-white channels on their TV. But to hear my cousin talk, well, the place was akin to Shangri-la, a mystical place that couldn't exist. There were never any bad moments, like having five ticks at one time on your back sucking the life out of you, or ripping your pants out in a mudslide and having to have six stitches in a very delicate place. No, none of those things ever happened.

When could a person's memory really be trusted? Was Marty Tarullo remembering a love between Anthony and Glory that wasn't real? That had been made romantic by time? Was Judy Pipkin's mother's memory correct? Or was she maybe a little jealous of the attention that Glory got? Had her memory of what happened become tainted with green? Or was her memory really the memories of her mother that she'd adopted as her own? I just couldn't be sure.

The most disturbing part of this whole existential epiphany that I was having in the most unlikely of places was that Colin was right. I couldn't go public with "theories" because then the public would start to come up with their own incorrect "memories" of what happened. I had to go public with facts or nothing. Right now all I had to give the public was the very things I hated. Random acts, misrepresentation, loose ends, and ambiguity.

Can I just say that I'm so happy that Colin wasn't anywhere around at this moment of weakness or I might have actually told him these things.

Then I got the phone call I'd been waiting for. It was Professor Whitaker. "Torie, you need to come up to my office. Emilia did this thing on her computer. She took pictures first with some digital whatchamacallit…Hell, I dunno, but anyway, she's been able to erase certain lines of the drawing, and I think she's got the face beneath the monster."

"I'll be right there."

I CALLED RUDY to let him know that I might be late. The college is almost two hours from New Kassel, and I didn't know how long I'd be there, so I wasn't sure when I would get home.

At one time southeast Missouri, like St. Louis, had been almost all French. You can still find a lot of French influence there, if nothing else in the last names in the white pages and the number of Catholic churches. In St. Louis, the French dominance is all but gone save for a few place names like Chouteau Avenue and a few sculptures like the one of Saint Louis at the art museum. The Irish, the Germans, and eventually the Italians came in and all but squashed the French.

West of St. Louis, along the Missouri River valley, was where the Germans mostly settled, followed by a good contingent of Irish, and it has remained remarkably

German. The area I am in has been called the Little Rhineland, and with all the excellent wineries that have popped up to dot the Missouri River almost all the way to Jefferson City, the title isn't far from correct.

Nestled in this amazing green, rolling countryside, Oldham College sat stoically on a hillside, facing south. In front of the building that houses the history department was a man-made pond filled with Canada geese and mallard ducks, all swimming, oblivious to my presence. Professor Whitaker was with a class when I arrived, and I had to wait fifteen minutes until he was finished. Then he led me down a hall, up a flight of stairs, and around a corner to Emilia's office. I could barely contain my excitement. Anticipation flowered in my chest as we entered the room where her computer sat with the monster face pulled up on the screen.

"Hi, Torie," she said. "I have to tell you, I've had a lot of fun doing this. I wasn't sure I'd find an image quite so clear, but here you go."

She pushed some buttons and explained what she'd done to obtain this image. Computer jargon. Me not understand computer speak. I just push buttons on a computer and things happen. When they don't, I call Rudy. When Rudy can't fix it, I call Rachel. If Rachel can't fix it, then we need serious help.

None of that mattered. Because when the computer was finished doing whatever it was it was doing…there was a face. Not a monster face, but a human face.

"Torie, are you all right?" Professor Whitaker asked.

"Why?" I asked.

"Because you just turned white," Emilia said.

"You're positive this is right?" I asked, feeling light-headed.

"Pretty dang close," Emilia said.

"Why, who is it?" Professor Whitaker asked.

"It's Sandy Kendall. Her father."

"Is that bad or good?" Emilia asked.

"It's not good."

TWENTY-ONE

I'D ASKED EMILIA TO FIND the human face under the monster face, but I thought she'd just uncovered the real monster. She printed a copy of the image for me. I thanked them both and left for home. I was in such a hurry to tell somebody what I had discovered that I just began making phone calls on my cell phone to whoever would listen. The first person I got was my sister, then Rudy. Then I called Colin and Mort, and neither of them answered any of their phones.

I arrived back in New Kassel around three in the afternoon and went to my office. Stephanie had left about a half hour before. I booted up my computer and then went to the kitchen for a Dr Pepper. The first drink was heaven. All that carbonation bubbling down my throat made me as happy as I could be, even if it was short-lived. The second drink was never as good as the first.

I went back to my office and pulled up what my old boss, Sylvia, had accumulated on the Kendall family. Many years ago Sylvia and her sister, Wilma, had decided to gather five-generation charts and family group charts on the people of New Kassel. They deposited them in the historical society so that people who wanted to trace their ancestry to this tiny town could find the information. I had spent many hours entering the handwritten documents into the computer, but I hadn't been alone. Helen had done some of it, Elmer had helped out, and on occasion even Sylvia had pitched in. Sylvia may have been a cold and cantankerous old bat, but she was light-years ahead of most of her generation, and she hadn't been afraid of change.

On more than one occasion these family group sheets and generation charts have helped me. On hundreds of occasions they have helped others connect the dots. At times, Sylvia had supplemented things she knew to be true with assumptions and her own memories. Those were the things I had to be careful of, because sometimes she could be a bit prejudiced. So I tried to keep this in mind when I looked up the charts on the Kendall family. I couldn't imagine that there wouldn't be information on them.

Sandy Kendall's five-generation chart indeed showed his ancestors back five generations, except on two branches for which Sylvia only had three generations documented. It was a pretty typical family tree of the "second boat" type. He most likely had no ancestors from the *Mayflower,* the first boat, but some lines of his family had been in the country since the 1630s or 1640s; thus they were part of the immigration wave known as the second boat. Mostly his family was from Virginia and Pennsylvania, with one line from Connecticut. Then I checked the family group sheets, which are a record of each person's family: who the individual married, children, and vital information, like occupation, place of burial, and birth and death dates.

Under Sandy Kendall's group sheet, Sylvia had written an addendum. Another page of nothing but notes. As I suspected, it was all about the suicides. As I had also suspected, Sylvia had known the family personally. She mentioned newspaper after newspaper coming to town to interview witnesses. Then in late 1993 she made just this one note:

Although these cases have long ago been laid to rest as suicides, I cannot help but think that in at least one instance, this is dreadfully wrong. I do not doubt that Rupert hanged himself from the tree in the backyard, as he was terribly deranged and ill from the trench warfare that he had endured. What that boy saw, nobody should ever see. How some men return from war intact and others don't is a mystery to me, but I think it has something to do with the state they're in when they go. Rupert had always been a gentle, almost timid soul. To think of him having to actually kill another human being…I'm honestly astounded that he made it home at all…. And, for the record, I am not at all shocked that Glory Anne would have taken too much laudanum, although I've never known her to use it. She was a friend of mine, although we weren't especially close. Glory Anne was not close to many people. But Rupert nearly tore open her heart. To see Rupert in that state was more than she could bear on most days. Then for Sandy to deny her the one true love she had—I think she'd hit bottom, as they say. She never spoke to me about planning to take her own life. She always smiled and acted as if everything was fine. I never expected she would do this, but when I heard the news, neither did it surprise me. Whalen is the one that I cannot fathom. Once Glory was gone, Whalen was free to find

Hazel. I suspect that is what he was about to do, but a bullet stopped him. Of course, I can never prove any of this, and I suppose it is unfair of me to write about their choices with none of them here to speak for themselves.

That was it. A few cryptic lines sprinkled throughout the paragraph that would drive me insane. I would think about them for months. Possibly even years, unless I learned the truth. Once Glory was gone, *Whalen was free to find Hazel.* What did that mean?

"What does that mean?" Colin asked from the doorway.

I jumped at his voice. "Oh, jeez. You scared me," I said.

"What does it mean?" he asked. He came in and sat in the chair across from me. He glanced at the Rose of Sharon quilt hanging on my wall.

"I'm not sure, other than I think I've been barking up the wrong tree this whole time."

"Explain," he said.

"Yeah," said Mort as he came in. "Explain for me, too."

"Oh, hi. I tried to call both of you and there was no answer."

"Looks like we both got the message at the same time," Mort said, smiling at Colin. "And here we are."

"Well, all this time I've been thinking that it was Whalen who killed Glory, although I could never come up with a really plausible reason why he would. Judy Pipkin's mother said that the brothers were crazy about their sister, and she implied that there was more to it than your usual sibling affection. So for a second I thought that maybe Whalen killed Glory because he didn't want anybody else to have her. That motive has never made sense to me, but the courthouses are full of cases where men have killed women just to keep anybody else from having them."

"Even some women killing men for the same reasons," Mort added.

"Psycho, but okay, it happens," I said. "And Marty Tarullo's story about Whalen bringing Glory Anne to break up with his brother—after you hear Judy Pipkin's story, it seems to fit. Whalen was forcing Glory to break it off with Anthony because he wanted her for himself."

"Can I just say this whole brother-sister thing is creeping me out?" Colin said.

"Yeah, me, too. But what I think happened was even worse. I mean, let's just suppose that the reason Rupert and Whalen doted on Glory and protected her so much was that they knew her father was doing the worst thing possible."

Mort and Colin looked at me blankly. It sort of made me feel good that they didn't immediately understand what I was implying. Finally, Colin said, "You mean, her father was molesting her?"

"I think so," I said. "Rupert was quoted as saying that he returned from the war to find a monster living here. He warned Glory Anne not to let the big mean man get her. Sandy was certainly a big guy, and I just came from the college, where an art historian showed me how she used her computer to restore part of the mural Rupert did on the wall. The part where the big Nosferatu-type character is trying to get his sister? You were right, Mort, there was another picture underneath. It was of Sandy Kendall. In Rupert's mural, his father, Sandy Kendall, is trying to devour Glory."

Colin and Mort exchanged glances. "But remember,

Rupert was not in his right mind. Maybe he thought his father was a monster for another reason. The war could have made him imagine all sorts of things," Colin said.

"He's got a point," Mort said. "What's your proof?"

I slapped my forehead with my palm. "Ugh. You guys and your proof," I said. "I don't have a big confession written in blood or anything, but Marty told me that Glory's father was okay with her marrying Anthony. He wasn't thrilled, but he didn't make any big fuss about it, either. So why did Sylvia write in her notes on the family group sheet that Sandy had denied Glory her one true love? Maybe behind the scenes Sandy was a bit more adamant. Maybe he even threatened Anthony, and maybe Whalen had told Glory to break it off to save Anthony. Sylvia also said, and I quote, 'Once Glory was gone, Whalen was free to find Hazel.' I've been under the impression that Hazel left because Whalen had done something terrible, possibly even because Whalen was in love with his sister. What if Hazel left because she found out what was going on with Sandy? What if Hazel left out of fear for her own daughter's safety? Hell, what if Whalen *sent her away* instead of her leaving? Then, obviously, Whalen never went to get her because he ended up dead. It would also make sense of why Hazel wouldn't have tried to get any of Sandy Kendall's money. She was afraid of him. She wanted to be far away from him."

Mort raised his eyebrow, and Colin leaned forward on his knees. "It's all speculation," Colin said.

"Not entirely," Mort said.

"What?" I asked. "What do you know?"

"I got the trajectory analysis back," Mort said.

"And?" I asked, swallowing hard.

"To cut out all the jargon, it simply states that somebody about six and a half feet tall shot Whalen while he was kneeling. Although we don't have an entry and exit wound to examine, Darla checked the rudimentary crime scene photos and the crime scene drawings, which did show at least the area of entry and exit. Still, without computer analysis of the entry and exit wounds, I suppose we can't be one hundred percent sure, but given the extreme angle of the splatter and Sandy's extreme height, I would feel comfortable saying in a court of law that Sandy Kendall, it would seem, shot his son Whalen while Whalen was on his knees."

I sat back in my chair and stared openmouthed at the new sheriff. Colin got up and walked around the room, stopping at the window to look out onto River Pointe Road. "So Glory and Whalen were both murdered," I said.

From the window, Colin said, "Glory was either killed by her brother Whalen to save her, or she was killed by her father so that nobody else could have her," he said. He looked me square in the eyes. "You realize we'll never know. Whalen's murder we can pin on Sandy, but Glory...I'm not sure we will ever know the truth."

"Okay, okay, okay," I said, "but why would Sandy kill Whalen? Do you think it was because Whalen knew about what he was doing to Glory?"

"Maybe it was because Whalen killed Glory," Mort said. "Like you said, Torie. It was a mercy killing. Whalen killed his sister so she wouldn't have to endure the abuse from her father, and when Sandy found out, he killed Whalen for killing Glory."

"I'm getting a big headache," I said. "Why didn't Whalen just kill his father? Why did anybody have to kill Glory?"

"Maybe he was going to," Colin said, "and Sandy just got to him first."

"Well, whoever it was," Mort said, "they both covered up Glory's murder. Either Sandy killed her and Whalen helped cover it up, or vice versa. Why would either one do that?"

"Again, we may never know," Colin said.

"I think Sandy had the most to lose," I said, "but I also think Sandy killed her. Because if Whalen killed her to save her or to put her out of her misery, why would he have chosen such a horrible way to do it, when he could have just given her laudanum for real? Whalen, if all this is true, would have been more humane about it. Sandy was angry. His property was in love with somebody else and he wanted her to pay. So not only did he pick an incredibly painful way for her to die, but he chose to administer that death with her most beloved thing, her quilting and sewing supplies. If Whalen was protecting her, he wouldn't have done that. He would have found a painless way to do it. No, that was Sandy Kendall's doing. Once he killed her, he panicked, thinking it might not look like a suicide, and he threatened Whalen with Hazel and Sophia to keep his mouth shut. I think later, when Whalen was going to go to Hazel, Sandy shot him."

It was quiet in my office. So quiet I could hear the refrigerator kick off down the hall in the kitchen.

"He couldn't take the chance that Whalen would tell," I added after a moment.

"Well," Colin said with a sigh, "I can't say that I disagree with you, but you cannot go public with any of this, because it is only speculation."

"I know," I said.

"You do?" he asked.

"I can lay out the facts we have, the documents we have, as part of the tour, but beyond that, my part in this story is finished."

Mort rose to leave and stopped in the doorway. "I'll deposit copies of the crime scene evidence with you next week. That way you can use them in the display when you open the textile museum," he said.

"Thanks a bunch, Mort. I really can't thank you enough."

"What for?"

"For believing me when I came to you with a wild idea."

"Gotta take chances in this world. I like a bit of a shake-up every now and then. See you around," he said and left my office.

That left Colin staring at the Rose of Sharon quilt hanging on my wall. "Is this one of Glory's quilts?" he asked.

"No," I said.

"How do you know?"

Well…I didn't know. "I just assumed it was Sylvia's. I thought maybe even Sylvia had made it."

"Maybe it *was* Sylvia's," Colin said. "Maybe Glory gave it to her."

"What makes you think it was Glory's?" I asked—although looking at it, I saw it could have been her work. I don't know why it hadn't occurred to me before.

He shrugged. "Hunch."

"Oh, you know what you always say about hunches," I said.

"I know, but sometimes they turn out to be right on the

money," he said. "Speaking of which…you did good work on this one, Torie. Really good work."

"Yeah, but you were right. You suspected Sandy back when I suspected Whalen."

"I know, but you figured it out. You corrected your own mistakes."

"More like I just fumbled my way through once I had enough evidence."

"That's all any of us ever do," he said. "I just wish you could have gotten your definitive proof."

"Are you feeling okay?" I asked him. He'd damn near given me a compliment, and he wasn't snickering or crossing his fingers.

"Call it distance," he said. "Once you put distance between yourself and the thing you do—or used to do—every day, it all looks different."

With that he walked out of my office. I was left staring at the quilt that had hung on my office wall for a decade or more and wondering if an alien had invaded the body of my stepfather. I stepped over and examined the quilt a bit more closely. There it was, down in the right-hand corner. The initials GAK, the year 1918. It had been hanging there all this time, and I never realized who had made it. Tears welled in my eyes, and I got the creepiest feeling that somebody was watching me. I rubbed my fingers across the stitches and sighed heavily. Well, I might not know for sure who killed her, but I now knew it wasn't suicide. I also knew what sort of private hell she had lived in.

The story of the Kendall "suicides" was finished as far as I was concerned.

THE NEW KASSEL GAZETTE
The News You Might Miss
By Eleanore Murdoch

Last weekend's rose show was a rousing success. Louise Callier's gorgeous Tropicana was the most outstanding rose in the whole show, in my book. However, many of you voted for Glamis Castle and Maddie Fulton's Graham Thomas. Don't worry, we'll educate all of you on the proper qualities of a rose before next year.

Congratulations to local historian Torie O'Shea, who has bought the old Kendall house for a textile museum. She hopes to have it open to the public sometime next year. If you have any old quilts or other textiles that you would be willing to loan to Torie for the opening of the museum, please contact her at the Gaheimer House on River Pointe Road.

Two nights ago somebody was seen leaving Velasco's Pizza with a woman who was not his wife. Please don't do that again, because I'm not so sure I can keep the secret next time. It's killing me.

Father Bingham wants to thank the local Boy Scout troop for collecting all those canned goods for the food pantry. Sam Hill wants to announce that Thursday night is ladies' night at the new microbrewery. He can't guarantee love or happiness, but he can guarantee good beer at cheap prices. And after that, who cares?

Would the unnamed individuals who are building

a shed in their backyard please stop hammering and sawing after midnight? The floodlights are really annoying, too.

Hope to see you all at the Strawberry Festival!

Until next time,
Eleanore

TWENTY-TWO

IT WAS JUNE, and the Strawberry Festival was under way. Every year we get more people driving longer and longer distances to attend. Parking starts out on Highway P, and some people walk as much as two miles just to get to the city limits. Wish I could take credit for all the strawberry jam, but I can't.

Rudy and I planned to close on the Kendall house July first. Word had gotten around already about the textile museum. I'd had many calls from people wanting to donate items. One woman told me she had one quilt that her great-grandmother had made, and rather than have her four children fight over it she was going to give it to the museum. To some extent, I found that sad, that it would be leaving their family. At the same time, I knew the quilt was less likely to get damaged at the museum, or lost, and the family could always come and visit it. No fighting or squabbling, and everybody would have equal access.

I pulled my car into the driveway of the Santa Lucia Catholic Church. I was here to do what I had promised to do for Marty Tarullo. As expected, he had died two days after I'd seen him in the hospital. I took my sunglasses off and set them on the seat next to me and stared out at the cemetery adjacent to the church. "I'll only be a minute," I said to Mary. "Stay in the car and watch your brother."

I grabbed the flowers that I'd bought and headed out to find Glory Anne Kendall's grave. Now that I knew whose grave it was, the striking sculpture of her nearly took my breath away. It was almost as if she were waiting for me, propped up on her side like that. There was a part of me that wanted to have her moved from this spot, away from her father. But then, why make her move when he was the jerk? I should have *him* moved. I wasn't even sure if the church would allow me to do something like that, but it seemed like a travesty for Glory to rest next to the man who had stalked her during life. Of course, maybe in the afterlife, it didn't much matter where either one of their bones lay.

I set the flowers in the built-in vase and had a moment of silence for her. I was overcome with wishing I had known her. I wished I had known the woman who had inspired a man to put flowers on her grave for eighty-plus years! A woman so unbelievably talented, who could create the most amazing works of beauty from scraps and some thread. A woman who was beautiful yet innocent, loving and admirably devoted to her mentally ill brother. A woman who gave away not just quilts but her time, and ultimately her love, for free with nothing expected in return. Anthony Tarullo had received that love, and had never gotten to marry her.

I couldn't say who I thought was the biggest victim in this whole thing. Rupert, the poor man, driven insane by what men can do to men? Whalen, forced to send his wife away because of what his father could do to his sister? Glory, a victim of a man's brutality, the ultimate act of betrayal? Anthony Tarullo, innocent of everything except loving Glory? Again, I was overwhelmed by the horrible things that people could actually do to each other.

Just as I was about to leave, I heard somebody behind me. Maddie Fulton walked up slowly with a cane in one hand and a pot of something in the other. "What are you doing here?" I asked.

"I want you to plant this rose on Glory's grave," she said. "It's a climber, and it's called New Dawn. Pink. Rather fitting, don't you think?"

I smiled at Maddie as she handed me the cutting of the rose. "I've got a shovel in the car. Don't you think it will look pretty when it's climbed up all over this sculpture?"

I had gone to see Maddie about a week ago and told her my suspicions about what had happened to Glory. "You know, I should have known when I saw the sculpture," I said. "Nobody has a sculpture made of his daughter like this. This is something a husband or a lover would have commissioned. Not a father."

"Well, we're gonna cover it with roses, so it won't matter," she said.

In the distance I heard a car door slam. Thinking it was Mary, I turned and saw Geena Campbell walking across the lawn. "I thought I might find you here," she said. "I wanted to tell you that in the bottom of Glory's sewing box, I found these papers."

"What papers?" I asked.

"Ordinarily, they would mean nothing," she said, "but in light of everything you've told me…I'd say they mean something."

She handed me the folded, yellowed pieces of paper, and I opened them with such trepidation that my hands actually shook. As I was about to begin reading, I saw another car pull up in the distance. It held Tobias, who stepped out and began walking toward us, holding a plant.

I read the pages in my hands. The first one read: *My father loves me. My father loves me. My father loves me.* Over and over in her loopy penmanship she had written those words. They must have been written a hundred times. The second paper read: *I am not a bad girl. I am not a bad girl.* Again, over and over, at least a hundred times. The third one said: *I love my father. I love my father.* Except somewhere in the middle of the page she had written: *Actions speak louder than words.* Then she'd repeated the *I love my father.*

"I don't understand," I said.

"I think her father made her write these."

"What, like sentences? Punishment? Like you do in school?"

Geena nodded with tears in her eyes. I checked the other two pages, and again the phrase *Actions speak louder than words* was written in the middle of the pages, among the other sentences. As far as I was concerned, this was my definitive proof. It wouldn't hold up in a court of law, but in my heart, I knew what happened to Glory and her family.

"Damn," I said, biting back tears.

"Yeah, double damn," Geena said.

"I want to plant this peony on Glory's grave," Tobias said as he approached us.

"Did you bring a shovel?" I asked.

"Of course," he said, completely indignant.

Behind him was Eleanore Murdoch. "Clematis," she said. "They complement roses really well."

So we all pitched in and planted the rosebush, the

clematis, and the peony, so that Glory could have flowers all summer long, not just in June. I'd still keep my promise to Marty. I would relish the simple act of coming here every June for an hour or two, remembering. I'd do it until I shuffled off this mortal coil or moved out of Missouri, and I don't expect the latter to ever happen. If I did, I'd recruit somebody else to do it. I'd do it because I'd promised— and because Glory deserved at least that much.

I SAT IN MY CAR on Haggeman Road, looking up at the Kendall house. It would be mine in a few weeks. Evan Merchant was busy carrying boxes out to the U-Haul truck. I wasn't sure what I was going to use his guesthouse for, but it came with the big house.

"Mom," Mary said.

"What?"

"What's for dinner?"

"Pickled pig's feet," I said.

"Mom, I'm not five anymore. That phrase is for little kids," she said.

"Right," I said, looking at her. She had her nose stuck in a comic book, and she hadn't a clue that I was watching her. Such a pretty girl, with a wide smile and huge eyes— and she wasn't five anymore. As much as I wanted to hang on to those younger years, I couldn't. I really did want her to grow up and become an adult and contribute to the world. I just knew that the more I let her and all of my kids go, the more it meant I was getting older and leaving this stage of my life behind. I wasn't ready not to be needed. I wasn't ready to be an afterthought in their lives.

I had to take advantage of every possible thing that I

could, because they were my contribution to the world. They weren't my possessions to do with as I wanted. They were their own people, with their own ideas, their own desires and dreams, and their own identities. The Kendall family had taught me that.

"Hey, Mary," I said.

"What?" she asked.

"You ready to color your hair?"

Her eyes snapped up from the comic she was reading. "You serious? Because you said before that you were thinking about it, but then…it hasn't happened."

"Let's go buy the hair color now," I said.

"Really?" she said. Her eyes sparkled with excitement.

"Yeah," I said.

"Black?" she asked.

I swallowed. "Black."

"Oh, you are the coolest mom in the world," she said.

Okay, I can live with that.